Acclaim for Alan Lightman's

REUNION

"Lightman's prose leaps and twirls, circles his subjects and raises them up. If Degas or Manet had written prose it would read like this." —*The Denver Post*

"*Reunion* seeks . . . to plumb life's most complicated and enduring relationship: that between who one was and who one is. . . . *Reunion* most powerfully explores the seductions and betrayals of young love." —*The New York Times Book Review*

"Undeniably affecting. . . . Memorably lovely. . . . Lightman's lyrical meditation on aging and nostalgia [will] hit home for just about any reader." —*San Francisco Chronicle*

"Haunting. . . . He has a Proustian concern for manipulations of time and memory . . . [a] melancholy grasp of the sovereign ineluctability of time, that 'hour of eternity.' . . . Such a rueful consciousness is a pleasure to witness." —*The Boston Globe*

"Prose both luminous and precise. . . . The images of lightness and beauty and grace, of complexity and obsession that Lightman conjures through Charles's vision of his lover make us participate in Charles's yearning." —*The San Diego Union-Tribune*

"A subtle and haunting novel. . . . In Lightman's hands, the act of remembrance becomes a meditation on time, loss, and the ultimate selfishness of love. His writing gets under your skin precisely because of its measured and undemonstrative tone."
—*Daily Mail*

"An achingly beautiful story about memory and the loss of passion. . . . Lightman succeeds in writing an inventive, unsentimental love story." —*The Star-Ledger*

"A profoundly human story, rich in depth and nuance. . . . Lightman writes with a lightness, a lyrical understatedness that belies the underlying depths and complexities of the novel. . . . *Reunion* is the work of a great writer." —*The Globe and Mail* (Toronto)

ALAN LIGHTMAN

REUNION

Alan Lightman was born in Memphis, Tennessee, in 1948 and educated at Princeton and the California Institute of Technology, where he received a doctorate in theoretical physics. His previous books include the novels *Einstein's Dreams*, *Good Benito*, and *The Diagnosis*, the collection of essays and fables *Dance for Two*, and several books on science. *Einstein's Dreams* was an international bestseller, and *The Diagnosis* was a finalist for the National Book Award in fiction. His latest book, a collection of essays, *A Sense of the Mysterious*, will be published by Pantheon Books in January 2005. Lightman's other works include research papers in physics and astronomy. He has taught on the faculties of Harvard and the Massachusetts Institute of Technology and is currently an adjunct professor of humanities at MIT.

REUNION

ALAN LIGHTMAN

Vintage Contemporaries

Vintage Books

A Division of Random House, Inc.

New York

FIRST VINTAGE CONTEMPORARIES EDITION, NOVEMBER 2004

The Library of Congress has cataloged the Pantheon edition as follows:
Lightman, Alan P., 1948–
Reunion / Alan Lightman.
p. cm.
1. College teachers—Fiction. 2. Loss (Psychology)—Fiction.
3. Class reunions—Fiction. 4. First loves—Fiction. I. Title.
PS3562.I45397 R48 2003
813'.54—dc21
2002034575

Vintage ISBN: 0-375-71344-1

Book design by Johanna S. Roebas

www.vintagebooks.com

Printed in the United States of America
10 9 8 7 6 5 4 3 2 1

REUNION

ONE

SHEILA lies on top of me, snoring, her heavy breasts heavy on my chest, her stomach on my stomach, her hair damp in the afternoon heat, a shard of light through the white shutters she closes when we make love, the slow beat of the overhead fan, the tiny sound of a radio from the street. I too am falling asleep.

I fly above mountains, dizzy, frightened. Someone's arm slides across my face. What? What? An hour has passed, maybe two. I sit up on the silk rug, sweaty. In slow motion, Sheila kisses the back of my neck, stands, and stretches.

"I like it here, with the books," she says and yawns. "I always have. Have you read them all? I'll bet most of them are for show." Grinning at me, she takes a long sip from the wineglass on the bookshelf. I watch the amber liquid swirl slowly around her lips, I stare at her body, creamy and white. She is not unattractive in her middle-aged nakedness, and I think that I may even love her, but I am ready for her to leave. There is a certain book I want to finish.

Still completely naked, she saunters into the kitchen and comes back to the study with the portable TV, turns it on. Click. We are watching a commercial about deodorant, then a news broadcast of some hurricane in Honduras. Hundreds of men and women huddle beside crude shelters, children play in the mud. Trucks unload food and medical supplies.

"I'm going to send them a donation," says Sheila.

"Them?"

"CARE. Oxfam. You should too."

What can I say to Sheila? I am still half asleep, limp from our lovemaking, unprepared even to look out the window. As I rub the sleep from my eyes, I am tempted to turn off the TV.

The truth is, I feel no connection to the faces on the screen. The Hondurans are just so many electronic pixels. I've decided that has been the great achievement of our age: to so thoroughly flood the planet with megabits that every image and fact has become a digitized disembodied nothingness. With magnificent determination, our species has advanced from Stone Age to Industrial Revolution to Digital Emptiness. We've become weightless, in the bad sense of the word.

The Honduran women in their earth-colored shawls, the vacant-eyed men wearing their lopsided straw hats, are nothing more than bits on the screen, surges of electrical current, evaporations. I wish Sheila had never turned on the TV. I'd like to drift back to sleep, or read.

SHEILA has been somewhere upstairs, rambling around in one of the rooms, and casually descends the long spiral staircase. She's put on a blouse but cleverly left it unbuttoned. "I'm going to send a donation." She raises one eyebrow at me, almost imperceptibly, waiting for me to say something or do something. I recognize this minute gesture as once belonging to my ex-wife. It was a sign that I was not paying attention. Unexpectedly, I find myself missing that little prod.

"You can afford more than I can, Charles," she says.

"Right." She is definitely trying to pick a fight. Could she be bored?

"Oxfam has an 800 number where you can use your credit card," she says. "Or you can write a check. To the

Honduran Hurricane Relief Fund. I'm going to write a check."

"Go ahead," I say.

Sheila looks surprisingly sexy with the unbuttoned blouse. Her body is real, her body is not a digitized bit, it has weight and it's twelve inches away. I reach for her breasts.

She takes a step back. "Don't act like a shit," she says.

I don't feel like a shit. I've thought about these things. Just the other day I was reading some article about the relativity of values. I mention this because it applies directly to the question of the Honduran hurricane victims on TV. Even if they are not mere electronic data points, those people are not nearly as bad off as they seem. Because well-being and need are purely relative concepts. There is no such thing as poverty in itself, suffering in itself, unhappiness in itself. All is relative. Galileo, the physicist, was the first person to understand this idea. Absolute motion is unobservable. Only the relative motion between two objects has any meaning.

The great painters also grasped the point: the eye responds only to relative lights and darks. Look at the pictures of Corot, for example *Landscape with Lake and Boatman* or *Château Thierry*. Look at the works of John Singer Sargent and Frederick Edwin Church. A dark region of canvas is dark only by virtue of being juxtaposed against a lighter region. Or consider colors. For years painters and photographers have known that the value of a color is perceived only in its relation to other colors around it. With the proper background, a green can appear brown, or a blue red.

According to whoever wrote the magazine article, and I cannot remember his or her name, it is only common sense to extend the argument to human contentment. Human beings consider themselves satisfied only compared to some other condition. A man who has owned nothing but a bicycle all of his life feels suddenly wealthy the moment he buys an automobile. For a few days he will drive his new car slowly through the neighborhood for people to gawk at, he will race his machine on the highway, he will lovingly polish the hubcaps until he can see his face in reflection. But this happy sensation soon wears off. After a while the car becomes just another thing that he owns. Moreover, when his neighbor next door buys two cars, in an instant our man feels wretchedly poor and deprived.

Now I think again of the Honduran hurricane victims, and at this point I admit that I am extrapolating the argument on my own, beyond what he or she wrote in the article. Who is to say that the Hondurans are needy or unhappy? Needy and unhappy relative to what? The fact is, they are probably not accustomed to having much. Aren't the Honduran children laughing as they play in the mud? To me, they look pleased as punch. Very likely they have what they need. Leave them alone. I can't decide what other people need, only what I need myself. But I'm losing the thread of my argument.

"Charles, I can see you thinking again," says Sheila as she applies dark red lipstick, using her little finger. "You're always thinking. It's not good for you."

I WRITE a check for fifteen dollars to the Honduran Hurricane Relief Fund and turn off the TV. Done.

Now we're eating ice cream, peppermint. Peppermint is my favorite, but I also stock plenty of pistachio and chocolate almond. Between bites Sheila draws on a cigarette and exhales in long silver strands. She wants to talk about a movie she saw last week, some romantic French thing directed by Jean Doumer. Although I go to the movies frequently myself, I haven't seen Sheila's film and can only nod while she talks. She leaves to get a second bowl of ice cream from the kitchen, I hear the fridge open and close, a spoon clinks on the counter. The movie will be playing for another few weeks, she says. Would I like to go with her Friday night? She wouldn't mind seeing it again.

For some reason I now recover the thread of the argument I was making before. The real point is this: I have come to understand my own modest needs and aspirations. More importantly, I have descended to the level I deserve. In the morning, before getting dressed, I stand on my porch in my pajamas for a few minutes and smell the new day before it slips through my fingers. I eat my two poached eggs (which I cook myself) and my dry piece of toast. I drink my cup of coffee made in my dripomatic machine, two spoonfuls of milk, no sugar. On weekdays I bicycle to my leafy little college, where I teach my morning classes. I make a few phone calls, meet a few students. In midafternoon I cycle home, past the well-tended gardens, the mailboxes on cedar posts, the two-story houses with their garages. Then I am home, in my own two-story house.

Actually, not my house. A small-college professor, living as I do on a small-college professor's pittance, couldn't afford this house by a mile. My ex-wife bought the house, then left it to me upon her departure. One of my less pleasant colleagues once sniffed at me: "Not all of us are lucky enough to have wives who leave us such splendid houses when they divorce us." And I answered, "It doesn't bother me one bit, partner. Perhaps you'll have better luck yourself the next time around." Barbara knew exactly what she was doing. When we split up, she took only a little porcelain bottle that we'd gotten together in New York. Left me the house, the car, all of the furniture, even her clothes. She should have taken her goddamned stuff. She should have taken the house. She got her revenge.

So I cycle through the neighborhood of successful lawyers and doctors and bankers, arrive home, and grade juvenile papers. In the late afternoon I fix myself a drink, take out a book, sit in my chair. After dinner I work on one of my five-thousand-piece jigsaw puzzles of the country-side of France. Some evenings I don't feel like working on a puzzle.

Wouldn't my life be ridiculously extravagant to a Honduran, flood victim or not? Of course. The main thing is: I don't want to be disturbed. I have made sacrifices for this effete life of mine, at least relatively speaking, and I am comfortable. Do I lead the life of a selfish shit? So be it. I am content in my shithood.

"Are you going to your college reunion thing?" asks Sheila. She is putting away her monogrammed cigarette case. "When is it? Isn't it in two weekends, on the sixth?"

"Yes. Will you go with me?" I realize now that for at least the last month I have been hoping Sheila will go with me. I went to my twentieth reunion alone, just after my divorce, and it was murderous. Everyone was paired up with wives and girlfriends. Guys from all over the country who haven't seen each other for twenty years, haven't stayed in touch, don't have any particular fondness for one another, crammed together for a weekend and acting like family. Then I skipped the twenty-fifth, the big one, the one where everyone talks about their place in the world. Out of the blue, I have decided to go to the thirtieth, all of us now in our fifties, balding, becoming farsighted, jowls beginning to sag, the precise knifeblade in time when we have accomplished much of what we are going to accomplish in life and are just beginning to stare at the black pit waiting for us at the other end. Why have I decided to go? I don't know. I don't know. But I am comfortable, I will say to my classmates, extremely comfortable. I don't want to be disturbed.

"I can't go with you," Sheila says. "Why don't you ask Emily?"

"Emily doesn't like to go on trips with me. She says that she feels like a child when we go on trips together. I probably won't see Emily until she comes home next Thanksgiving. Maybe not even then. Maybe she'll spend Thanksgiving with Barbara."

"I wish I could go with you. But I've got a client meeting that weekend."

"Please go with me."

She hesitates. "Maybe I can reschedule the appointment." She looks at me sympathetically from across the room. But she has hesitated a few seconds too long, and I can tell that she doesn't want to go.

"No," I say, "don't reschedule your appointment. It's all right." Why can't people be honest with each other? I am not being honest either.

Two

THE book I want to finish reading is the biography of a minor German astronomer named Ulrich Schmeken. Written by Ralph Cunningham, one of my college roommates of long ago, who will be attending the reunion and will almost certainly want to talk at great length about his book. Cunningham's biography is out of print. The copy I have he sent me years ago, and I just recently peeled it out of its shrink wrap from some small university press.

Here is the essential story: Schmeken worked in the late nineteenth century at an observatory in Heidelberg. His specialty was discovering asteroids. Schmeken carried out his research by himself, but some nights when he walked up the hill to the observatory, he would take with him one or another of the young women from the village. Under the silver dome, he would light a few candles, share a glass of wine with his awed feminine companion, undress her, and make passionate love to her. Then, in the remaining hours of the night, Schmeken peered through his telescope in search of new asteroids. Among Schmeken's recorded discoveries are Asteroid Catrina 1894, Asteroid Eva 1894, Asteroid Ilsa 1895, Asteroid Winifried 1895. Cunningham describes Schmeken's observatory as shaped like a woman's breast.

The biography then takes a momentous twist. On a mild autumn evening in 1898, one of Schmeken's young ladies refused to join him in preasteroidal coition. The astronomer begged. Of course he would name an asteroid after her. But she would not budge in her virtue. Evidently Schmeken had never been turned down. He was so defeated that he walked out of the observatory that very night, never to return to his scientific career. The unconquered young woman, on the other hand, went on to become a distinguished biologist.

Much of Schmeken's story is known because the astronomer carelessly kept a personal diary in the same journal as his astronomical observations and annotations, all mixed together, a highly unprofessional practice but a gold

mine for Cunningham. "23 April 1895, $10^h03^m4^s$ (pm)::
Object E at ra $11^h32^m47^s.8$, dec 3°14'11"—Offset from
AG13: ra $1^h13^m36^s.2$, dec 4°17'34"—Mag 14.8. Hope to get
a third sighting tomorrow night. . . . Anna is even more
lovely than I thought. She has a small mole on her left thigh
and asked me to kiss it over and over. I in turn . . ."

To this particular passage, Cunningham, as fastidious
as I remember him in college, adds a tantalizing footnote:
"Schmeken does not use the common German word for
kiss, *küssen,* but the unusual word *lecken,* meaning lick. In
my judgment, Schmeken intended in this context to mean
kiss, and I have translated the word in that way." My own
reading is that Schmeken, in his observatory, made eros
from science.

It seems that the unconquered young woman, named
Lena Hammans, also kept a diary and provided her own
description of the fateful night. At the beginning of the evening, Schmeken was gracious and gentlemanly, placing his
cloak on the bench for her to sit on, letting her gaze eagerly
through the telescope, comparing her eyes to a planetary
nebula. But at her refusal to take off her clothes, he went
mad. He went wild. He stomped his feet, he screamed, he
grabbed her by the hair, he began throwing precious astronomical lenses and eyepieces to the floor. She was shocked
that a man of science could act in such a way, until she un-

derstood sometime later that sex is the most powerful force in the universe. And she was the master of that force. With such a realization, she decided that her own science was to be biology, not astronomy or physics.

CUNNINGHAM has been obsessed by Schmeken's story for years. So obsessed that he suffered through an astronomy course at the age of thirty-five while writing his book. I agree that it is a story of great sadness. The astronomer, although he behaved badly, was a tragic figure of sorts. He allowed his personal pride to end his promising professional career. And there lies the tragedy. Yet the interesting question remains: Was it personal pride or simply raw sexual frustration that caused him to go berserk that night in the observatory?

Perhaps Schmeken did not appreciate his own needs. Surely he must have needed the satisfaction of his scientific career, he must have needed his self-identity as a scientist. But perhaps he needed more his identity as a man, defined in terms of his command over women. And here a single failure, relative to all of his successes, proved fatal. Whereas a lesser Casanova, that is, an ordinary man, would have been accustomed to occasional demurs by the opposite sex and not reacted with such violence and finality.

I do envy Schmeken's passion. I look over now at Sheila, at her hazel eyes, and wonder if they are the color of planetary nebulae. I look at Sheila and realize that she and I never had much passion between us. Our conjugations have always been halting and measured, as if from memory. As if that is how people of our age should make love.

There is more of the astronomer's story. Thirty years later, when he is in his seventies, living infirmly but quietly in the countryside, he writes a letter to Lena Hammans, the famous biologist, apologizing for his conduct that night and asking forgiveness. She does not answer him. He sends her a second letter, painfully worded, which she ignores as well. Instead she prints both of his letters, in full, in her memoir, *Meine Laufbahn*. She mocks Schmeken, even when he is old and feeble, and exalts in her position. For she has made a discovery far more important than any of his pebbly asteroids. She has discovered the most powerful force in the universe, and that force is all the stronger for not being diluted with compassion.

THINKING of Cunningham, I remember another of our college classmates, Nicholas Blanchard, now a well-known military man, who sometimes went drinking with us when he was not in his ROTC uniform. Nick enlisted in ROTC because they paid his tuition, but he had a deep mistrust of the military establishment, as did most of us in the late 1960s. Having his college tuition paid by the ROTC, Nick said, was a way of "using" them, of getting even with them. His ultimate intention was to subvert the organization, and it was easier to subvert from within. To further insult the organization, Nick often wore a brassiere under his uniform, expecially to drill practices. (Several times a week the cadets marched up and down the soccer field in full dress.) Nick would come back from drill practice with a smirk on his face. I wondered how the ROTC could be insulted if they didn't know they were being insulted, but Nick insisted that the hidden insult was the best insult of all.

After graduation Nick continued to use the military. He rose through the ranks and became, at age forty-four, a brigadier general, just in time to serve in the Persian Gulf War. A week before the war began, with ships and planes hovering at the borders of Iraq, when the whole world was questioning whether the United States had the nerve to unleash its armaments, General Blanchard uttered in front of the cameras the line that would immortalize him forever: "You don't think that President Bush is going to let us step up to the plate without taking a swing, do you?" I saw all of this on CNN. Nick, is that you? Could that be you? Are you wearing your brassiere?

The Nick on TV wasn't any more real than the Gulf War itself, a made-for-TV war, a video game, another digitized disembodied nothingness like the Honduran hurricane victims, created to sell deodorants and premium beers and cellular phones. On my sixteen-inch television screen, red boxes neatly circumscribed bomb targets. Smoke puffed out of hoses backstage, miniature buildings shook and crumbled on the set. The only interesting thing about that war was Nick's announcement in front of the world's cameras: *You don't think that President Bush is going to let us step up to the plate without taking a swing, do you?* When did Nick start using baseball metaphors? Nick never knew beans about baseball, or any other sport.

The story later came out that the infamous statement wasn't initially the brigadier general's idea. In fact, brigadier generals weren't supposed to say anything at all to the press. Some higher-up, a two-star, had it in for Nick and challenged him to utter the line, thinking that it would get him thrown out of the service. Challenged his manhood in particular. Because Nick did have a soft voice. But after the infamous comment to the world press, things changed in Nick. His voice became brassy. He developed a swagger. I believe that he pictured himself as a war hero, even though he went back to Cincinnati for the duration of the war (probably watching it on TV). Nick was always a coward.

REUNION

A FEW years ago I ran into Nick by accident at a hotel in Chicago. I was attending a meeting of the Modern Language Association. I don't know why Nick was there. He was dressed in uniform, two aides hovering around him like bridesmaids. An aide for each star on his shoulder. Of course, he'd been promoted, despite the Gulf comment. We met in a crowded, dimly lit lounge, with muted blue cushiony chairs and couches and tapestries on the wall. Nick nodded, clearly recognized me but couldn't immediately come up with my name, said hello so faintly that I couldn't tell if he'd said anything at all. Then he did remember my name, asked about where I was living, what I was doing. As we sat down together, he suddenly said, in a loud, magisterial voice: "There is not a lot to love about this country." Pause. "But I do love the freedom."

"Yes, freedom," I said. Nick looked at me. For a moment, I flashed upon a horrific hunting trip I had taken with him, years ago. He'd organized the expedition so that he could shoot some unauthorized rifles. In my memory, I could hear the rabbits scream, see them lying ripped and bleeding. I found myself angry at Nick all over again. Then, unaccountably, I wanted to share something personal with him, something of me, something I'd accom-

plished with my life. I took from my wallet a recent picture
of Emily, who had just turned twenty-one. "My daughter,"
I said, and placed the photograph on the arm of Nick's
chair.

He looked at the picture. I believe that he smiled. He
may have been about to trade a photo of his own, but he
was caught up in the momentum of what he was saying
about freedom. "Do you know what freedom I love most?"
he asked. He leaned over to me, so that his medals swung
away from his chest. Despite being close, his voice billowed
and boomed, so that everyone could hear him. I was like
the interviewer on camera, the ear for the world. Nick leans
over to me and says, "I love it that Americans have no responsibility. That's the greatest freedom of all. That's what
we need to protect." I may be paraphrasing, but those are
the words I remember.

One of the aides, the one holding Nick's hat, gazed at
the brigadier with total veneration. But I was puzzled. Was
Nick being a complete cynic, or was he serious? Many of
the people in the lounge were also puzzled. Glasses clinked
nervously. Everyone was squinting at Nick in the dim room,
squinting under the single chandelier that threw out tiny
pinpoints of light.

"But, sir?" said one of the men standing in the lounge.
Sir? How do you address an important military man when

you don't know exactly what all of those stripes and gold insignias and medals connote? You could say *general,* but your man might be a major, or an admiral, or who knows. The public isn't trained in these things.

"But, sir? With due respect, you don't mean that, do you? All the citizens in a free democracy have responsibility . . ." And the man elaborated his objection, invoking the Revolutionary War, the Boston Tea Party, the Founding Fathers, the Constitution, everything else he remembered from his high school American history class.

At this point a woman wearing a skimpy black dress and a diamond necklace interjected: "Excuse me. I think I saw you on television in the Gulf War. Didn't you say something about getting up to the plate and swinging a bat? General Blandguard? Are you General Blandguard?"

"General Blanchard," said the aide holding the hat. That aide stood up. Nick remained sitting. Now the people in the lounge inched closer to him. The center of attraction had been apparently identified and was even more important than they thought, although not necessarily important in a favorable way. I heard grumbling, some nasty comments.

Then Nick rose hugely from his chair. He stood a few moments, as if to say something, but he seemed unsure about what to say. I could see hurt and confusion in his face. Then he walked out of the lounge.

One of the aides followed. My last memory of that scene was watching Nick walk out of the room, wondering what he was feeling at that moment, and then turning to stare at the aide left behind, who was now fondling the hair of a pretty young blonde. For that aide, probably a lieutenant or something in his twenties, all of the subtle politics and offended honor of the last moments had barely entered his peripheral vision, so focused was he on seducing the blonde. We are all being seduced, I thought to myself.

I IMAGINE Ulrich Schmeken and Lena Hammans walking up to the observatory together, before the attempted seduction. It would be a clear, moonless night, the kind astronomers need for their work. He is wearing a cloak, she a shawl of some kind in the cool evening air. They hold a flickering oil lamp for light, they step carefully on a gravel path winding up the hill. She walks a couple of paces behind him, allowing him to lead, excited by the night, by the astronomer, by the silvery silhouette of the dome in the distance. Schmeken is not a handsome man. He is short, slightly bow-legged, with a crooked nose, a mouth hidden by a small dry mustache (but a mouth well capable of licking the alluring moles on a woman's thigh, and here I insist on the original language in Schmeken's diary, not Cunningham's wimpy translation). They have met a few weeks earlier, at the university library where she works cataloging books.

"What will you show me, Herr Schmeken?" she asks. There is a boldness in her voice. That she addresses him first, without waiting for him to address her, is already a sign that she may not be as passive as his other young sparrows, but he doesn't register this dark hint, he is pleased at her initiative.

"I will show you Saturn, and the Andromeda Nebula." Saturn, embraced by celestial rings. He wants to take Lena's hand, she has such delicate hands, and hair that cascades in dark waves like the dark filaments in Orion. (He hasn't yet thought of comparing her eyes to a planetary nebula.) Hesitating a moment, waiting for her to catch up to him, he inhales a scent of her hair. What is that mysterious smell? Cinnamon? Lavender? Divine. Her hand brushes his hand, skin against skin, and an electric jolt goes through his body. How he wants to hold that hand as they walk up the gravel path to the observatory, but it is too soon. He must approach her slowly, slowly. He must woo her. All of the cards are in his favor, except for his lack of good looks, but what are a man's looks beside his achievements and personal machismo? He is the wise older man, is he not, the man of science, privy to the intimate secrets of nature, able to unclothe the heavens themselves. The dark shapes of trees, swaying slightly in the smooth evening breeze, seem like bodies offering themselves to him. He has the cards. He will be patient.

"I would like that, Herr Schmeken," she says. She gathers her shawl more tightly around her shoulders. "But I want you to explain what I have read in the books. Will you explain to me?"

"Yes," he says and smiles at her. She is his. He would like to kiss her now. Even beneath her shawl, he can see her breasts straining at the fabric of her dress. He would like to lick those breasts. But he will have to wait a while longer. And afterward he will obtain a critical position of Object K with the elongated orbit, his new asteroid, the one that will make him famous. He is in ecstasy. Lena's breasts, the new asteroid, Lena's breasts, the new asteroid. He is so dizzy with emotion that he can barely stay on the path.

To take his mind off his condition, he begins talking, saying anything. "Who was that woman I saw you with at the library last week?" Did he see her with a woman at the library? He can't remember.

"It could have been Sylvia," she says sweetly. "She's the librarian for foreign books. Was she tall?"

"No, she wasn't tall." He can barely think. Tall, short, he doesn't care, he's only moving his mouth.

"It might have been Brigitte, then."

His heart is pounding. And he has a colossal erection, making it uncomfortable to walk, a telescope in his pants. He cannot talk anymore. He can think only of licking her breasts. And afterward the asteroid.

HERE I must digress to face head-on this difference between kissing and licking, an issue that I did not raise myself, remember, Cunningham raised it in his footnote, but I must respond. Because now that I think more about it, the difference between kissing and licking is not a small thing. It is the difference between leisurely romance and fierce passion, between cold and hot, between stone and blood, between mind and body. Isn't it true that we kiss with our minds but we lick with our bodies? We kiss grandparents, children, too-familiar spouses. Kissing can be polite, a peck on the cheek, even a full kiss on the mouth, even the French kiss (which, in its use of the tongue, begins to approach the genuine lick). But licking is never polite. Licking is ill-mannered, licking is total surrender to sex, total surrender to body, to animal need, to flowing juices. Licking is the return to primality.

Most critically, a kiss can circumvent the tongue while a lick cannot. And it is the tongue, not the genitals, that is the primary sexual organ. Sade, in the third section of his *Philosophie dans le boudoir*, makes no less than eleven references to *la langue* (the tongue). I am quoting now from a junior thesis by one of my students, devoted entirely to the tongue in erotic literature. According to my student—and she did a great deal of research—eating and speaking are, in fact, minor functions of the tongue. The major purpose of the tongue is for sex. Someday evolutionary biologists may prove this assertion. Eliminate the tongue and sex is in jeopardy, it is possible that advanced life on earth might never have taken hold, evolution might have been stopped in its tracks. Not that higher animals without tongues would have found it impossible to reproduce, but they would have had no inclination to do so.

Some of these speculations seem absurd, I acknowledge, but not completely absurd. One thing is clear: Nothing is more sensual, more sexual, more arousing than *tasting* another person's body. And on the other end, receiving the humid caress of the tongue, which can travel slyly to places where no other explorer can go. Listen to Valentine's lines in Shakespeare's *Two Gentlemen of Verona: That man that hath a tongue, I say, is no man, if with his tongue he cannot win a woman.*

Schmeken—no, I must now call him Ulrich, I feel now on a first-name basis with him—Ulrich was a licker, I am certain of it. In fact, I believe that the distinction between kissing and licking lies at the core of understanding Ulrich, his needs and his behavior, his being. Cunningham didn't understand Ulrich at all. Unless there is some remarkable revelation in the last twenty pages of his six-hundred-page tome, Cunningham completely missed the point. I will have to speak to him when I see him.

BACK to Ulrich and Lena: they are walking up the hill to the observatory, which is now only a hundred yards away. They can see the small wooden door on the side, illuminated by starlight. He has a colossal erection, he can think only of licking her breasts, then the rest of her, making passionate love to her, and afterward the asteroid.

And what is she thinking? Appearances to the contrary, despite that she seems merely another of his pretty young creatures, she is in actuality far smarter than he, she is destined to become a distinguished biologist (of which fact she has no inkling at this time). She has consented to go to the observatory on this clear and moonless night because she wants to learn from him. The books in the library have stirred her mind. Probably she has dismissed the thought that the homely Herr Schmeken with his crooked nose and his little mustache, twenty-five years her senior, could possibly entertain any romantic intentions (much less intentions of the kind we have elaborated). To her, he seems harmless, a harmless man of science who can serve as her mentor.

But perhaps she is going with him under false pretenses. Perhaps she suspects his erotic designs and is actually using them to her advantage, pretending to be an innocent victim only because she covets his astronomical knowledge. Perhaps she is leading him on (it wouldn't be the first time), perhaps it is she who is controlling the moment. She will ask adoring questions, she might even allow him one kiss, but nothing more, then she will seize all that he has in that ugly cranium of his, she will excavate his brain. She will extract his scientific intelligence.

Poor Ulrich. Ulrich has gravely underestimated the young woman following two paces behind. All he can think of are heaving breasts and bright asteroids. He dreams of a night of two loves, women and science. He will make love to this woman and then to an asteroid. He has no idea that in another few hours his life will be bled dry, he will be the dried shell of a fly in a spiderweb.

THREE

PEOPLE mill about, chatting and drinking as we wait for the awards ceremony to begin. Someone has just sat down at my table with his wife and two daughters. Michael Bisi, his name tag reads. Michael peers at my name tag and offers his damp hand. I don't remember him at all. In his pinstripes and bow tie, he vaguely resembles a much trimmer French classmate named Renault, a champion squash player, but who could say what Renault looks like now, thirty years later. I was a wrestler myself, and my body has turned to flab, but turned to flab in its own special way.

Michael's wife, Louise, is a stout, scowling woman

with Brillo-like hair. Louise has scribbled in her own college on her name tag. "Here we go," she sighs. She takes off her sneakers and begins rubbing her red swollen feet. Immediately the teenage daughters head for the far end of the table. The girls wear sleeveless sundresses and high heels and cast condescending glances at the male student waiters.

Looking at Michael's beautiful daughters, I wish that Emily had come. She doesn't even know I'm here. I wish Barbara and I had conceived more children, maybe one of them would have come with me. My eyes wander through the crowd searching for someone I know, past the tables and beer kegs to the edge of the tent, where I see an unfamiliar brick building. So much of the campus has changed since I was last here. I feel exiled from my own past.

Every minute some classmate walks up to Michael and pats him on the back and then exchange business cards. How's the shoe business? No complaints, Michael answers. See you've moved into Philadelphia, someone says. People wear shoes in Philadelphia, Michael answers and grins. He's about to put stores in Los Angeles and Houston. Michael, bulging in his pinstripes, smells of expensive cologne. As each person walks by, he looks down at their shoes to see if they are brands that he sells. Florsheim, Bass, Johnston and Murphy, some fancy Italian outfits.

Michael is smiling, but I think he is smiling too much. I am about to tell Michael that I am extremely comfortable myself when he stoops to the grass and begins examining my own shoes, brown wing tips I bought years ago. He squeezes the toes, then pokes at the sides of my feet. "These aren't shoes I carry," he says, frowning. "I'm not sure what they are. But I'd like to give you some advice. You need better arch support. I haven't fitted shoes for a hell of a long time, but I still know how to do it, it's like riding a bicycle, and you need better arch support. You can believe me on that."

"I've been wearing these shoes for years," I say. "I'm not in the market for new shoes."

"You're ruining your feet," says Michael. "Next thing it'll be your tendons start to give you trouble, then your back. It's all connected." Indeed, I've been having back trouble for two years, but I won't give Michael the satisfaction of telling him. Michael stands up, grunting with the exertion, and wipes the sweat from his fat face. He himself is wearing Nike running shoes. "Like walking on air," he says when he sees me looking. "Jesus, I'm hot. Are you hot? It's got to be body heat. There's a lot of people in this tent." He takes off his jacket and hands me his card.

"I'm not in the market," I say again. Michael is a pusher.

"Nobody said you're in the market," says Michael. "All I said was, you're ruining your feet. And I didn't say anything about style, did I, but you can tell a lot about a person from the style of his shoes." He takes another glance at my feet. "Ever see stand-up pictures of Ronald Reagan? He wore cap toes, usually black."

I am beginning to dread that Michael will sell me some shoes before the long night is over. And I'm exhausted from my six-hour drive. I eye nearby tables, but all the seats are occupied. Another family now sits at our table, another unrecognizable classmate with children and an extraordinarily young wife or girlfriend. She could easily be his daughter, but she has her hand on his thigh in an unmistakable way, and they've kissed more than once. Now a band is setting up amplifiers in the corner of the tent. The guitarist plays the first crazy notes of a Jimi Hendrix song.

A CLASSMATE I see on occasion, Tom Zwicker, passes by and says hello. His face has a pucker that it didn't have the last time I saw him. "You're alone?" asks Tom. I nod. "Bummer. Jenny didn't want to come?"

"I broke up with Jenny three years ago," I say. "You?"

"Sorry about Jenny." He pauses. "October'll make twenty-five for Mary and me. Andrew just graduated from college. Wants to be a doctor, like his dad. Kara is a senior in high school. It goes by, doesn't it. I'm chief of surgery now."

"Congratulations," I say.

"I saw that article you wrote for *The Washington Post* a few years ago. Great. Who were you quoting? Shakespeare, I seem to remember. Shakespeare and affirmative action. You academics are always bringing Shakespeare into everything." Tom laughs heartily.

"What's wrong with Shakespeare?" I say.

"Don't worry about it. I was making a joke." Tom laughs again. "What else have you published? Did you ever publish any of your poetry? I remember your poetry in *The Pig*. Quite good. Let me know when something else comes along. I'll be on the lookout for it." He holds out his beer cup in a vague toast and walks back to his table. Screw him. I'd like to know what Tom's published.

"I'm not wearing this thing," Michael's wife, Louise, suddenly says. She rips off the pig's snout from her face, slaps it down on the table, reaches behind her back, and pulls off the curly pig's tail. "Keep yours on if you want to."

"Come on, Louise," says Michael. "Be a good sport." He looks wounded, as if Louise has committed an act of disloyalty. Michael and I are both wearing our snouts and tails. All of us are wearing them, in orange and yellow, the college colors.

"I agree with Mom," says one of Michael's daughters, at the other end of the table. She removes her snout and tail and drops them into a puddle of beer. "The pig thing sucks. Why couldn't you do a lion or a zebra or something like that?" Her cellular phone rings, and she answers it, speaking secretively into her purse. She reminds me of Emily.

An undergraduate waiter, wearing a snout and tail, comes by our table with a pitcher of beer. His voice is drowned out by an announcement of the first award, for the man with the least hair. A dozen guys leave their cheering families and go forward, their bald heads slick and shiny under the floodlights on the tent poles.

"Louise," says Michael.

"What?" mumbles Louise. She doesn't look up from the magazine she is reading.

"I want to go out with Ronnie and some other guys tonight, later. Is that okay?"

"Do whatever you want," Louise says. "I don't care."

Michael turns to me. "Would you like to hear how I got started in shoes?"

HE came from Italian immigrants, Michael Bisi tells me, his father was poor, his grandfathers were poor. All in retail, but they never made a cent. Clothes, hardware, automobile accessories. The family never made any money. Always they had piles of unsold inventory in the spare room of the house. At night they ate canned beans and canned corn and pasta for dinner. In winter they closed off most of the house and slept on the linoleum floor of the kitchen with the stove going. Michael was smart, he got a scholarship to college, and his father told him that this was the last hope for the family. Or marry a woman with money.

In the end he didn't marry for money, Michael says, he married for love, and he's had a wonderful marriage ever since. He looks over at Louise, buried in her magazine. No complaints, he says. People do worse. In college he took a business course and then opened a small store a few years after graduation. First hardware, like his father's father had done, then shoes. A distant cousin loaned him the money. One day Michael saw a picture of some new Italian shoes in a magazine and was suddenly gripped with an inspiration. Top quality was the key, not stocking too much, keeping good records, following the seasons. Then he got someone to manage his first store and opened a second, working fifteen-hour days. Now, lo and behold, he has twenty-seven stores.

I think Michael's saga has finished. But he adds an unexpected detail, an afterthought, as if he wants to correct an impression of having led a predictable life, or perhaps because he wants to impress the other classmate at the table, who has been stroking the backside of his twenty-two-year-old girlfriend while giving Michael and me looks of condolence. There was another woman before Louise, Michael says. He pauses. A young woman he met in his mid-twenties when they were both visiting Boston. Why is Michael telling us this? I feel embarrassed for him. He met her by accident at the entrance to a park. They spent part of one day together. It was May. They walked around the park, that was all. She (Michael doesn't mention her name) lived in California and had to go home. She wrote him a letter. Michael answered her letter with a telephone call. They talked for a few minutes. After hanging up, he realized that there were certain things he had wanted to tell her but hadn't. Some weeks went by, he became busy with his new store. They never spoke to each other again.

Now Michael is finished. He adjusts his pig's snout and takes a long drink of beer.

No one has been listening to Michael's story except me. And I was not interested myself until he got to the end, the only part I believe. Eating canned beans and corn, sleeping in the kitchen for heat? Come on, Michael. I don't believe it. That's just too noble. A heroic mythology, an invention you've been telling your family and friends for years, undoubtedly embellishing along the way. And the wonderful marriage? Look at your wife. She's bored out of her skull, not just bored with this reunion but bored with her life and with you. She has boredom and contempt written all over her face. I can picture what she does each day while you're traveling to Los Angeles and Houston. After the girls go off to school, she waits for the mail at the end of the long drive-way. She watches *Days of Our Lives* on TV while she puts pink nail polish on her toenails.

But the last part of the story—the part about the young woman you saw for a day and then never again, perhaps the only woman you ever loved—that fleeting bit has the texture of truth. That is a true tragedy. An opportunity lost, a life thrown away. You might have been happy with the woman from California. I believe that you've been thinking of her ever since. Why else do you remember her? And maybe she's been thinking of you too all of these years, thinking of that one day in the park. And now she is in her fifties, probably married with children, far past her bloom.

I ASK myself: Could Michael have known on that warm day in May, years ago, that a critical turning point was at hand? Momentous choices constantly bombard us, but we are usually unaware of them at the time. On that spring day in May, without warning, Michael's life gushed into a break point, like a river rushing to the mouth of two branching channels, splitting, half flowing into one channel and half into the other. But the junction was sudden, and Michael didn't realize he'd made a turn until very far downstream. Could he possibly have tested both channels, then paddled upstream to choose the happier path? But the current was too strong. Time flows only one way. I seem to remember Kierkegaard or somebody saying that life can be understood only looking backward, but it can be lived only going forward.

No, Michael Bisi could not have known at the time that he flowed into the wrong branch of the stream. Louise, with her Brillo hair and permanent scowl, was waiting. In fact, Michael may still be deluding himself into thinking that he took the best path. Or he may be telling himself that it doesn't matter, that nothing ever lives up to our hopes. Wasn't it Calvino who said that desires are already memories?

It is clear that Michael is unhappy, but either he does not know that he is unhappy or he has accepted his unhappiness. Yet if he is oblivious to his unhappiness, why did he tell me the story?

Perhaps it is simply nostalgia. All of us here are watching the world grow older.

AND your story? Michael asks me, smiling.

Again I study his smile, and this time I can see the sadness behind it. The woman from California, I want to whisper to him. Where is she? Does she exist? She must exist, she must. I imagine Michael and her in their walk around the park, their single day together. They have just met, by accident, but instantly they know that there is something between them.

Pale tulips border the winding stone path, velvet in the afternoon sun. A pond, flowering trees above their heads. Their slow steps on the stones are like someone faintly knocking at a door. Isn't it the future that knocks? After a few minutes, they hold hands. (Unlike Ulrich, he is not playing a card game; unlike Lena, she does not feign shyness.) Is it unusual that a man and a woman begin holding hands after knowing each other for ten minutes?

In fact, Michael and the young woman from California are themselves surprised to be holding hands so soon, surprised by what their bodies have done, and agitated. It happened like this: They are walking side by side, exchanging a few words. He looks at her, then away at the trees. She looks at him. A breeze lifts her hair. Their hands brush against each other, unintentionally. Without thinking, she shifts her purse to the outside shoulder. He gazes at her again, steps an inch closer. She allows her body to drift slightly toward his. Their hands touch again, just the outsides of the hands, between fingers and wrists, only a gentle touch, but they both hold the touch. They no longer look at each other, they do not want to acknowledge the secret of their hands touching. Then, a few moments later, he discovers that his fingers entwine hers, hers entwine his.

Michael and the young woman are tingling. They know that something has happened, although neither is remotely aware of the branching channels ahead. Her eyes are the color of sky. She is studying medicine, she says, and she plays the flute. He tells her about his family, his new shoe store, his dream to own twenty-seven shoe stores. What makes a good shoe? she asks him. She has no interest in shoes, but she doesn't know what else to say, and she doesn't want to reach the edge of the park. She feels herself churning inside. She wonders if he is churning inside too, but he must be, he is holding her hand, isn't he? Or is she only imagining his hand holding hers, just as I am now imagining her? She concentrates on that single point of contact, their fingers touching each other. She can almost feel his pulse through his fingers. She is living completely in that bridge of their bodies, his hand in hers. He is so gentle and sweet and sincere. How can these sensations occur after only a few minutes? A few minutes ago she was intending only to rush through the famous park with the swan boats on her last day in Boston, just a quick walk through the park among strangers. Now she begins wondering if she should postpone her return trip to California, miss the next week of her classes. But that would be reckless. What could she be thinking?

On and on the two of them flow, closer and closer to the branching channels ahead.

Michael, she is there, she is there. Can you see her now, twenty-five years downstream? Does she exist? If I can imagine her, she must exist.

AND your story? Michael asks me. Didn't he ask me that question before? I have not been paying attention. I look down and see the tiny reflection of my face in his large ruby ring. I am comfortable, I say, extremely comfortable. There, at last I have been able to say it. The reason I am here. Now I can go home, back to my comfortable life. I find myself disturbed by everyone here, disturbed by Michael's wrong turn, disturbed by Tom's ridicule of my writing, disturbed by the loud Jimi Hendrix pounding my head.

A new award is called out, for the man who has been divorced the greatest number of times. Our neighbor with the chesty twenty-two-year-old girlfriend raises three fingers, but he doesn't win. He is tied with a half-dozen people. Someone is quadruply divorced. The victor takes a bow, to applause, and receives his certificate. The announcer shouts: "Longest citation in *Who's Who in America*." Someone has thirty-seven lines. "Best preserved." This category proceeds by popular vote. Several classmates have annoyingly retained most of their hair and their firm stomachs. They stride up to the middle of the tent. They are asked to take off their shirts, and they oblige. Wives and girlfriends make comments, begin telling lewd jokes.

FOUR

SATURDAY morning, the memorial service. Sun streams through the stained-glass windows of the chapel and pours wandering paintings onto the wood floor. A hundred and fifty of us classmates sit cramped together in stiff chairs. The chaplain is pale, a ghost in a house of ghosts. "The nation has changed since June of 1969," says the chaplain. "Those were troubling times. The spirit of the nation was troubled." He begins reading the names of the classmates who have died in the past thirty years. With all the glass and the smooth plaster walls, there is an echo in the chapel, and I hear each name twice. As if the second canceled out the first, birth canceled by death. The chaplain pauses between names, the echo makes its erasure, a life comes and goes in a few seconds.

One of the deceased I remember, Robby Talbot, gone at age forty. I can see his red hair and freckles and bright eyes. Robby kept a strange map on the wall of his dormitory room, a map of a place that didn't exist, an island in the shape of a hand. Its fingers splayed into the sea. Such a lengthy, convoluted coastline was impossible to defend, Robby said, and many countries had invaded the island, Remidia, Tiberine, other imaginary lands I no longer remember. But there was nothing of value on the island, so the conquerers always departed. On the map Robby had drawn valleys and mountains, lakes and forests, and labeled each with a beautiful curving script, in black ink. His handwriting was delicate.

AT lunch, eating hamburgers, corn on the cob, buttery mashed potatoes, and cole slaw, I spot Cunningham across the courtyard. He has set up an autograph table, piled with dozens of copies of his biography, but no one is standing in line. Cunningham sits alone and forlorn at the table, nearly hidden by the stacks of thick books.

"Ralph!" I call out to him. His eyes light up. Three pens

carefully placed on the table are ready for service. Would I like to buy a copy? No, I already have one, he sent a copy to me years ago, doesn't he remember?

"But you never reviewed it," he complains. "I thought you occasionally reviewed books."

I am not going to argue about reviewing and proceed directly to my main point. "It's licked, not kissed," I say.

"What are you talking about?"

"Ulrich Schmeken and the young women."

"You read it then?" he asks hopefully. He seizes upon a pen, as if ready to autograph my copy. But I don't have my copy, I left it at home.

The thought occurs to me that I may be the only person on the planet who has read *Ulrich Schmeken*. With this re-alization, I don't have the heart to tell Cunningham that in my opinion he missed Ulrich Schmeken completely. I pull up a chair and sit beside him.

Of course Cunningham wants to talk about his book. Indeed, he is exploding with his book, as if he had written it yesterday. An odd fellow, Ralph Cunningham. He doesn't fathom the profound difference between kissing and lick-ing, he has not grasped the full sensuous passion of his bi-ographical subject, and yet he himself is passionate about his book. He has dedicated his life to this book, both while writing it and long afterward, even as the hundreds of unsold copies sit gathering dust in his basement. Cunningham has, in a way, lived a life brimming with passion. I wonder if he has ever been equally passionate about a woman.

"I am writing a new book," says Cunningham.

"About what?"

"About Ulrich Schmeken. Some new letters were recently found in the home of a grandnephew in Munich."

WE sit together talking for another half hour, remembering certain things from our college days, but still no customers for *Ulrich Schmeken*. Classmates begin wandering off to the afternoon events. With a sigh of resignation, Cunningham abandons his table, and we start a slow walk around campus, he happy to be in the company of a man who has read his book, and I fascinated and perplexed by his enthusiasm for the new project.

In a few moments we pass under the stone arch of the courtyard and then out along the diagonal path to the gymnasium. A building I look for has burned down, another has been remodeled so drastically that I can hardly recognize it. A new dormitory, a new student center where there once was a garden, a row of trees in the place of a stone wall. The college has changed. Silently we walk along the pebbled path, both moving by habit, taking latitude and longitude from the memory of arms and of legs.

Under the shade of a giant white oak sits a familiar stone building whose cool interior promises relief from the sun. We enter. Cunningham is saying something about a trip Ulrich Schmeken took to France. As he walks toward the sound of a billiards game down the hall, talking over his shoulder, I am half listening and half looking for the Trustees Room, which I remember to be in this small building. And I find it, dark and wood-paneled and smelling of lemon oil. Here I am alone. Rare books hide in a recessed alcove. Against another wall is a model of the college, not the campus today but the campus of decades ago, as I knew it. Here's the Baston Arch, where the Piglets sang "Take Me Back," the stone wall near the college store, the twin Prytaneum and Tholos, which I admired on my way to classes. There's Thayer Hall, the spindly McMillan House with dripping age stains and secondhand bicycles leaning against its Gothic stone front. Newton, Livesey, the chapel, and across the grass courtyard, Brandenberger Library. I lean down and peer into the windows of the library. I can see microscopic students sitting in the reference room, microscopic books piled on rolling trays, a clock. On the miniature pathways and walks, I spot students I remember from long ago, tiny, Nick Blanchard, Wayne Manning, Phillipe Renault. Trees, a smell of damp leaves in the air. A cloud drifts through space.

And there, sitting cross-legged under a tree between Davis and Smith halls, I see myself. My books lie scattered on the ground. I hold in my hand a letter from a young woman. In the courtyard below, two students dressed in shorts and orange and yellow T-shirts play Frisbee, but I do not see them. The chapel bell chimes the hour, but I do not hear it. I stare at the letter and remember her eyes. I look up from the letter, a breeze tosses my hair. I look up and gaze at the crisscrossing walks, the leaded glass windows, the stone carvings where I have been happy these past several years. She remembered, she wrote to me. I turn my head, I stare up, I sense a vast white. Looking down at my miniature self, I wonder if that tiny young man can see the big me. The wind picks up a hat and carries it off, across the courtyard, past Davis into College Place.

The young man who is me brings the letter to his face. The soft beige paper has her smell. He was sure that she would forget him after that brief conversation in the coffee shop. Instead, she has invited him to come watch her dance. He thought he would never see her again. Wednesday. He'll take the eleven A.M. bus to New York. He'll cut his American Poets class.

HE thinks about her all during biology lab, his single science requirement, which he has postponed and postponed until senior year. The unpleasant class takes place in a gigantic basement, filled with metallic instruments and stone tables and rows of dirty sinks, fiercely illuminated by overhead fluorescent lights, smelling perpetually of denatured alcohol. The professor is never there, leaving only the cheeky teaching assistant to answer questions.

Charles stares at the glass slide under the microscope. White blood cells. Red blood cells. All flattened and lifeless, when he is feeling so alive. He imagines her in a sexy ballet leotard, tiptoeing across a red and white checkered floor. Music in motion. She glides, she twirls. A lily nestles like a small bird in her hair. She turns and gazes at him, her audience of one, alone in the front row. She beckons. And then, miraculously, he is dancing with her. He leaps through space, scissoring his legs. He holds her lightly around the waist as she spins and floats in white air, her silkiness brushes his face.

Somewhere he hears himself dictating nomenclature to

his lab partner. *Mitochondria. Vacuoles. Cytoplasm.* The names are the one and only thing he likes about this class. He loves the sounds of the words, the sheer textures and images. *Pneumococcus.* He feels a soft, moist, enveloping cloak. *Homeostasis.* The *st* sound cuts through the air like a knife and eliminates all that is not certain in the world. *Endoplasmic reticulum,* his favorite. He could repeat it forever. Endoplasmic reticulum. The soft syllables of *endoplasmic* gently oscillate like waves rolling on a beach, then are rudely diverted into deep winding troughs by the *reticulum. Reticulum, reticulitis, reticulosos.* He invents and imagines. Another name: *fibrils.* He pictures delicate little forest animals, darting behind bushes, vanished before seen. They hop, they play, they make tiny high-pitched cries.

"What the fuck are you doing?" says Malcolm, his pimply lab partner. "I'll take the scope and you record."

"Okay," says Charles.

Malcolm rudely seizes the microscope, upsetting the focus, looks over his shoulder, and scowls at their classmates a few lab benches away. "Hold it down, you weenies and potheads, this is serious shit we're doing here." The target of his reproach: A half-dozen students have abandoned their scientific investigations in favor of passing a joint back and forth with dissection tweezers. Between drags, they loudly debate the meaning of "Lucy in the Sky with Diamonds." Tangerine trees and marmalade skies, bellows the teaching assistant. It's all fruit. Fruit. Bullshit, another student says. Unplug the smoke detector, moron.

Someone hands Charles the joint. He hesitates, thinking of his lab notes to write up, his history paper, wrestling practice in a few hours. Yet he hates to be regarded as the self-righteous bookworm. To smoke or not to smoke? That is the question. He has approximately six seconds to make the decision before everyone will notice that he's brooding over another decision. What should he do? How long has he been holding the joint? Now the saliva-soaked paper has burned to the edge of the tweezers, which are growing hot in his hands. He begins to pass the marijuana without smoking, changes his mind and brings it to his lips, then changes his mind again.

"Lunchtime, Charlie," someone says.

"I'm just preparing my mouth," he says. He takes a hit and passes it on.

Juliana. Two days until he can see her. How can he survive until then? These past three years his romantic life has been a desert. Something must be wrong with him. Something is wrong with him. He is too timid, he is too serious. He is witty, but his is a slow wit, and he never thinks of the clever response until the moment has passed. Lisa, his obsession of junior year, stopped returning his calls after three dates. Had he burned his draft card? Lisa asked him one evening. If she were a guy, she announced, she'd burn her draft card. Two days later it came to him what he should have said: If he were a girl, he'd demand to be subject to the draft.

He's starving for female company. Why is this need so great? When he was younger, in high school, he thought that he could bury himself in his books and be content, like Emily Dickinson, who, despite a few passing infatuations, lived within herself and by herself, almost her entire life in a single brick house. *This ecstatic Nation, Seek—it is Yourself.* His need confuses him, humbles him, confirms that he is only an animal after all. He is a cow, a dog, maybe even a worm. A victim of biological evolution, not in control of his own body or life. Does this mean that E.D. was not flesh and blood? Was she some superior being?

Ribosomes. Lysosomes. He vaguely hears. He copies down the words, syllables not words, in his illegible handwriting. Somewhere a bottle of soft drink is pried opened and spews like a geyser. Followed by a flood of laughing and giggling.

Juliana. Juliana. A name more mellifluous than any biological term. He loves the sound of her name. It has a foreign sound, a self-alliteration, Italian possibly, or maybe Spanish. But the J would then sound like an H. Those magical few moments in the coffee shop in New York, after her morning class. Her bare arms were glistening with a soft sheen of perspiration. Her cheeks flushed. Straw-colored hair fluttered around her face like sunlight on water. And she wrote to him, she invited him to watch her dance.

But what if she is only toying with him? What if this is how she amuses herself, inviting young men to New York to gallop and pant after her? Maybe the address that she gave him doesn't exist. Maybe the address will turn out to be a warehouse or a deserted apartment complex. After spending two hours on the bus to New York, he'll find himself walking around some condemned building, broken glass crunching under his feet, nothing in his heart except the prospect of a two-hour trip home. It's happened to him before.

He hates this need for feminine intimacy, this need has caused him only misery, and he wishes he could cut it out of himself. His few groping sexual encounters have fled from his body within hours, leaving no trace. And then the misery again. He suffers, as all animals suffer.

Juliana, the lovely ballerina Juliana. Juliana, be mine. He will write her a poem. Flipping to a back page of his notebook, he writes down a word of passion, crosses it out, and writes down another word. What can he possibly say of his heart? A word. Only a single word. A single syllable.

WHAT? What the hell is going on? Am I hallucinating? I must be dreaming. I've got to sit down.

I must have had too much beer at lunch. How many glasses did I drink? Two? Three? Or maybe I'm disturbed. Yes, that must be it. I've let myself become disturbed. And now I'm imagining things because I'm disturbed. I never should have come to this disturbing and vicious reunion. It's time to go home. I'll leave tomorrow morning, first thing.

Juliana. Yes, I remember. Everything.

HE continues composing the poem in his American Poets class. How would E.D. do it? *Love is like Life—merely longer.* That would be a grand opening, and he admires E.D.'s perennial theme of immortality. But he is not yet in love with Juliana. More importantly, he does not want to seem presumptuous. And certainly their acquaintance of sixty minutes has not reached the point of eternity. He has been in her presence an hour. An hour of eternity. An hour of eternity. Yes, an opening line! *An hour of eternity.* Not the premature profession of love, not a magnification of the actual passage of time, but a metaphorical statement.

The literature professor, James Galloway, paces the aisles between desks as he lectures, stopping now and then to sweep back his fashionable shoulder-length hair. Galloway is a man in his early forties, handsome and dashing, but with heavy eyelids and a cloud of sadness hanging over his head. He pauses to glance at Charles's scribbled lines, nods, and moves on.

Charles is not unhappy that Professor Galloway has seen that opening line. *An hour of eternity.* Perhaps the professor will agree to discuss it after class, or in his personal study where he occasionally invites students. Unconsciously Charles pictures his visit to Galloway's home the previous winter, a cold evening in December, everyone's boots squeaking and crunching in the snow as they walked from their cars to the professor's front door. Inside they sat in a circle on the floor of the study, discussing literature and smoking marijuana, calling repeatedly to Galloway's wife in the next room, but she wouldn't join them. Then Galloway, stoned with his pupils, read aloud his own unpublished poetry, which was surprisingly melancholy and sentimental. Charles senses that he shares something with Galloway, some kind of dissatisfaction with life.

At this moment Galloway seems to be launching an unorthodox and upsetting interpretation of Emily Dickinson, causing Charles to look up from his poem.

"Dickinson was antiestablishment before antiestablishment, revolutionary a century before Ginsberg and Ferlinghetti." Galloway pauses, as if waiting for his contemporary references to win the attention they deserve. "'Safe in their Alabaster Chambers,'" he reads aloud,

Untouched by Morning
And untouched by Noon—
Sleep the meek members of the Resurrection—
Rafter of satin,
And Roof of stone.

"Does anyone know who 'the meek members of the Resurrection' are?" Silence. Charles never responds to these rhetorical questions, when Galloway knows the answer. He will not be the guinea pig. But he will listen and observe what Galloway has to say. Although Galloway is irreverent, he is also brilliant, and Charles wants to learn everything he can from his teacher. The professor slows his stride by the desk of a particular student, leans down, and says, full of goodwill, "Jonathan, who are 'the meek members of the Resurrection'?" Jonathan shrugs.

"Timothy."

"People who rise from the dead," says Timothy, rubbing the side of his face. "I'm not sure. Ask Jonathan." There is sluggish laughter from the class. Some students are still hungover from the weekend.

"Let us not be too literal," says Galloway. He taps a pen against his desk and waits patiently for an elaboration that everyone knows will not come. A fleeting touch of sympathy passes over his handsome face. Such vacant minds, he must be thinking. Minds for him to fill up, not just with poetry but with life. "I would argue," he says, "that the 'members of the Resurrection' here could be Christ's followers, of course, or members of the Church, or authority figures in general. And Dickinson is suggesting that this authority is impotent, sleeping through history as time marches on, locked away in stone coffins. Not just locked away but 'safe.' Safe. She is mocking authority."

The professor pauses again, inviting further comments. Charles will bide his time. He is paying close attention now.

"And consider the last line of the poem: 'Ah, what sagacity perished here!'" For a moment Galloway turns and stares at the trees outside the window. Perhaps he is lost in thought, or perhaps simply overcome with his own analysis. "A truly sagacious authority would never sleep while the world happens. Dickinson is being sarcastic here, isn't she. She in fact means just the opposite. She suggests that the Church, or the Authority with a capital A, or the Government with a capital G, is a fool." Galloway makes a small bow of his head and strides back to his desk, his Guatemalan sandals clapping softly on the wood floor.

Charles can contain himself no longer. Galloway has gone too far. Emily Dickinson was not a revolutionary or a cynic, she was simply a free spirit, a deeply spiritual person, as Charles will show in his senior paper. He raises his hand and is called on.

"But if the sagacity perished," Charles asks, "how can it be sleeping? The members of the Resurrection and the people who constitute the sagacity cannot be the same group." Simplicity itself. His is not a vacant mind, to be filled with Galloway's long hair. The air hangs heavy with the incisiveness of his question. Maybe he will be a professor of English himself someday, like Galloway. Or, better yet, a poet or a novelist. All of his professors have told him that he has the makings of a fine poet, that he is destined to be a professional writer. For two years in a row he's won first place in the college creative writing contest. How he wishes Juliana were here with him at this moment, hearing this challenge to Galloway.

"Good point," says Galloway. "Would anyone like to respond to the comment?"

A student in the back of the room, a graduate student

who is doing his doctoral dissertation under Professor Galloway and sometimes sits in on Galloway's undergraduate classes, speaks without raising his hand. Everyone turns around in their chair to observe the speaker. "Dickinson surely doesn't mean that the sagacity *literally* perished," says the graduate student. "She's speaking metaphorically, of course. The sagacity perished in terms of losing its effectiveness, its power."

"Right," says Galloway.

That is all. Crushed in a word, a single syllable. Charles has been too literal, he sees it now. What could he have been thinking? Stupid, stupid, stupid. But still he objects to Galloway's reading of E.D. Galloway is in one of his outrageous moods, and he's getting away with it. If only Charles were smarter, he could find the flaw in Galloway's ridiculous reading.

"Everyone, I assume, knows Wilder Pritzke, in the back," says Professor Galloway. "Mr. Pritzke has just coauthored with me a paper on last lines in three Robert Frost poems."

I T seems that a copy of the document in question, fresh from the typist, has just found itself on the professor's desk. Galloway lofts the paper into the air, a salute to his student. In doing so, he inadvertently glances at the title page. A shadow passes over his face.

"What's this? Wilder Pritzke and James Galloway?" The words seem to have tumbled from his lips unconsciously, inappropriately.

"What is what?" says Mr. Pritzke in the back of the room.

"Nothing," says Galloway. "It's nothing."

"But you said something." Pritzke rises from his chair, a tall, thin young man with bloodshot eyes, dressed like an unmade bed. Charles can see his hands shaking. "You read out the authors of the paper, didn't you? Pritzke and Galloway. What of it?"

Galloway smiles. "I thought we had settled this," he says softly. There is regret in his voice, almost a poetic melancholy, as if he has been through some terrible and private travail. "We will talk about it in my office after class."

"No, I want to talk about it now," says Mr. Pritzke. "Do you have a problem with the names on the paper?"

Galloway carefully folds the manuscript and places it beneath a stack of books on his desk. He is back in control. But it is evident that he will have to say things he'd rather not say. He looks up at his young charges, suddenly most attentive. He looks at Mr. Pritzke. "It is just that we agreed my name would go first on the paper," he says gently. "We agreed on this last week. You must have talked to the typist since then, didn't you." He pauses. "Unless there is a strong reason otherwise, alphabetical order is the normal order of names on academic papers." This last comment he makes not to Pritzke but to his students, as if in a mini tutorial, as if he were explaining the definition of *synecdoche*.

"But in this case, there *is* a strong reason otherwise," says the graduate student. "I did most of the work."

Galloway seems hurt by these words. He smiles with embarrassment. But is he embarrassed for himself or for Mr. Pritzke? The professor hesitates, searching for the right words. "Putting aside the question of who did most of the work," he says, and now he pauses a very long time, as if to clearly suggest that he does not at all accept Pritzke's claim, indeed Pritzke's claim is absurd, but Galloway will not stoop to the pettiness of debating it. Or perhaps he does not want to humiliate Mr. Pritzke. "Do you remember the paper by Gertrude DeMille, Robert Farley, and Jennifer Eggers, on Sandburg? A few years ago. In *Journal of New Literary Criticism,* I believe. Mr. Farley's name went first, and everyone thought Gertrude was overly promoting her student so that he could land an assistant professorship. People were extremely suspicious. Farley didn't get a single interview at the MLA that year. It would have been far better if Gertrude's name had come first, in alphabetical order."

"With all due respect," says Pritzke, "that's not the same situation." He has taken a step toward Galloway's desk. He is not smiling like Galloway, but he is not quite as sure of himself as before. "There were three authors there. And I think it was Farley, DeMille, and Eggers on the title page, not alphabetical and not reverse alphabetical. That calls attention to itself. Farley, Eggers, and DeMille would have been no problem."

"I believe you are mistaken," says Galloway. "It *was* Farley, Eggers, and DeMille."

Mr. Pritzke is thinking. "Wait a moment," he finally says. "DeMille could be alphabetized with the D, or with the M, as in de Mille. Stanley de Camp, for example, is always with the Cs, I'm sure you know. If it's the same in this case, your argument doesn't make sense." At this juncture, Mr. Pritzke walks to the blackboard and writes "DeMille," draws a line through it, and writes "de Mille" beneath it.

"I fail to follow you," says Galloway. "If de Mille were with the Ms, then Farley, Eggers, and de Mille would still be neither alphabetical nor reverse alphabetical order." Now Galloway goes to the blackboard and writes: "Farley, Eggers, de Mille." The chalk makes an excruciating squeak. He then lists all of the possible orderings of the three names, including lower-case ds and upper-case Ds. The sound is unbearable.

The graduate student seems confused. "It was Farley, DeMille, and Eggers," he says, retreating to his first statement.

"Do you know who David Levy is?" asks Galloway.

Pritzke's face loses focus, as if he is going through a list of all known literary academicians in his head. Galloway continues: "What many people unfortunately do not know is that David Levy chaired an international session of the IAS in 1963, examining the question of the order of names on academic publications. The committee's findings and recommendations are published. You might read them. Thanks to Professor Levy, there should be no argument about these things."

Pritzke rolls his bloodshot eyes. "With all due respect, I am not about to grovel in front of the so-called recommendations of some asshole committee, pardon the French, that knows nothing about what we are talking about here. We are talking about fairness. We are talking about student-teacher power monopolies. We are talking about hierarchies and class systems. It was you who brought up the, quote, Farley, Eggers, and DeMille paper. It was you who misquoted the order of names. It was Farley, DeMille, and Eggers. Your argument doesn't hold water."

Galloway sighs, a grand lamentation. He seems to be suffering from so many things, Charles thinks, but perhaps he *wants* his students to see that he is suffering. After a few moments, Galloway installs himself in his chair, places both hands on his desk, palms up, and lightly closes his eyes. "I'll tell you what," he says finally. "The order of names on our paper will be Pritzke and Galloway. How is that?"

The class is stunned with Professor Galloway's seemingly magnanimous gesture. Pritzke is stunned. In one sentence Galloway has conquered the day, demonstrating more clearly than ever that Pritzke's claim was unfounded, demonstrating Galloway's own graciousness and nobility. But he is wounded. Everyone can see that he is wounded. Or pretending to be wounded, Charles can't tell which. In silence Galloway gathers his papers. While he is doing so, the Smith clock tower begins chiming. The class is over.

CHARLES hurries to catch up with Professor Galloway, who is walking quickly down the stone steps and out into the courtyard. It is raining. Galloway seems gray and alone in the rain, a King Lear who has just been betrayed by his own flesh and blood. Charles calls out to him. Galloway, now halfway across the diagonal path, turns and waves him off.

"'An hour of eternity,'" shouts Charles through the dark shudder of rain. "Do you like it?"

"I don't have time now," Galloway shouts back. He is still walking away. "What is it?"

"The first line of a poem I'm writing. To a girl."

"A love poem?" Galloway stops. "Don't ever write love poems." Then he disappears in the rain.

FIVE

CHARLES has twenty minutes to get ready for wrestling practice. He enters the common room of his dormitory suite, says hello to Wayne and his sixteen-year-old girl-friend, Missy, who are both lying on the dusty green couch and fondling each other.

"So, what's happening?" Wayne says in his habitual half-mocking tone. He slowly raises himself on his elbows, thick and glazed, as if surfacing from a sea of molasses. Wayne is hugely muscled, with widely spaced eyes and long, scraggly blond hair. He wears a T-shirt saying "Fuck Me," blue jeans ripped so that his underwear shows through in the crotch and the butt. Caught off guard by her lover's change in angle, Missy suspends her affections, looks admiringly into Wayne's eyes, and then relocks her body with his.

"Wrestling," says Charles.

"Tough boy," Wayne says in a muffled voice. "Honestly, you guys are tough dudes. I mean that. I don't have the guts to get my shoulder dislocated three days a week." Without displacing Missy, he carefully extends an arm and turns on the stereo. *Purple haze was in my brain, lately things don't seem the same.*

For a moment Charles stares enviously at Wayne and his girlfriend, then looks away. Envious, but not envious enough to get entwined with sixteen-year-olds. For the last month Missy has been sneaking over every afternoon after her classes at the local high school. Any day now her parents could find out and get Wayne thrown out of college, or sent to jail. But then again, Wayne's got a lady and Charles doesn't.

"New guy on the Croak-a-Bloke board," says Wayne, pointing to the tacked-up list of names he keeps of recent graduates killed in Vietnam. "Guy named Ellis Morgenstern. Did you know him?"

"No." Charles vaguely remembers the name, an editor of one of the student publications.

"Graduated two years ahead of us."

An hour of eternity. The words now seem so theatrical. Maybe Charles should abandon the poem altogether. His poetic urges, so strong a few hours ago, are curiously waning. He will never be a writer, he will never be a man loved by women. In fact, he can't imagine himself being anything. Suddenly he is empty and miserable again, that familiar sensation that takes away all desire to move.

"Why don't you and Missy go into your room," he shouts over the music.

"Jack's there," says Wayne. "And besides, we like it out here." Missy giggles. "Are we bothering you?"

"No, do whatever you want. I'm leaving anyway."

"Hey, I'll bet you're the only poet on the wrestling team," says Wayne. "Am I right?" Charles doesn't answer. "Course I'm right. I know you got two engineers. Any black guys on the team?"

"No black guys."

"Course not," says Wayne. "Do you know how many black students we have on the whole campus? I looked it up. Twenty-five. That's less than one percent."

"Shit."

"Shit's right. I'm joining the Black Panthers. And I want somebody to write to my mommy and daddy and tell them. Will you do it? Write a poem to them about my joining the Black Panthers."

"I forgot," says Charles. "You engineers only learn how to write numbers." Wayne does this. He's trying to be funny to impress Missy. But Missy doesn't need it, she's already plenty impressed. Charles looks at her quickly and notices that she's sweaty and beautiful.

"Be nice," Wayne shouts over the music. "I'm getting out of this place."

"What about me?" says Missy.

"I'm serious," says Wayne. "Bobby Kennedy. Martin Luther King. They can shoot me next. But I'm not getting killed in fucking Vietnam. This country is full of shit. I'm joining the Black Panthers. They take white guys."

"Stop talking," says Missy.

ON the wrestling mat, he tries not to think about his life. Concentrates only on torso positions, arms and legs, places to grab and leverage his weight for a takedown. In five minutes he is covered with sweat, dripping on the mat. The wrestling feels good, even the pain where his arms have been wrenched. He is in his body now. A whistle blows. The other guy, a teammate, is a couple pounds heavier but not as fast. Charles lunges in the shot, grabs a leg, flips his body. Someone hollers nearby. He disengages, grips again. His body is moving now, his body is a powerful machine, with not just power but speed and cunning, he is thinking only about moving his body, leveraging his weight. It occurs to him that he is writing a poem with his body, a poem of brutality and truth. *An hour of eternity.* Who needs eternity? All that matters is this second, the force of his body. Muscles, sinews, flesh. Graduation doesn't matter, or the year after, or the uncertain profession after that. He'll probably be drafted anyway, sent to crazy Vietnam, land of flame, maybe he should have burned his draft card after all, moved to Canada like some of his friends, he's a coward, he doesn't know what he believes. The vague unwillingness of his future stretches to infinity in a zillion grains of sand, tiny syllables. He won't live that long. Even tomorrow doesn't matter. Or the next hour. All that exists is this second. Maybe even a second is too long, a second can be subdivided into a thousand slivers of glass. He exists only in a sliver of a second. Red drops speckle the mat like a red falling rain. A nosebleed, or the slice of a fingernail that should have been cut. Now they are down in the wet red. His eyes whip by the bleachers, rows of unoccupied seats. He is occupied. He twists, he grips, he forces. He doesn't even care about pinning, he is a machine, not an animal but a cunning machine. He forces, grinding his teeth against the mouth guard. Someone cries out, his guy maybe. He only tightens his grip, forces harder, harder. Screams again.

Why don't you pin him? somebody shouts. Forces harder and harder. The screaming is drowning his mind, soothing his mind like sweet wind. He lets go. He lets go. He lets go.

That evening he visits the library. Showered and calm. He loves the quiet of the library, the hidden reading rooms lit by brass lamps, the walk home through the college grounds late at night. Tonight he leaves with a book about ballet. He crosses the campus, listening to the soft sound of his steps, and enters a side door of the physics building. Down the weathered stone steps to the basement, to the end of a corridor, and the dark storage room, the secret place. Inside, he lights a candle and closes the heavy steel door. Silence. Strange objects flicker on shelves, glassy, metallic. A coil of wire glints and winds around a curved bell. His book flickers, a glossary of terms, which he is trying to memorize before Wednesday. *Arabesque. Battement. Batterie. Bourrée. Cabriole. Cambre* . . . He imagines her body making each movement, as quick as the light. Divine Juliana. Fill his body and his soul.

SOMEHOW it continues, this persistent dream. But I'm awake, I know that I'm awake. I touch a wall. I touch my face. Why am I standing in this place, watching this hallucination?

But . . . there I was! That was me. I was magnificent. I had completely forgotten. I was beautiful. My body when I was wrestling, that was me, my body, shining with perspiration, so strong and muscular and . . . magnificent. I had forgotten. And young. Could I ever have been that young? Not a wrinkle in my forehead. Not a crease around the eyes. A thick scalp of hair, broad shoulders, erect posture. Flat, lean stomach. It makes me want to cry. Let me sit down. I was merciless with that guy on the mat. To be honest, I could have let go sooner. I should have let go sooner. I was a cruel SOB. But it was a wrestling match, wasn't it. You inflict pain in a wrestling match. You hurt, and you expect to be hurt. Keep in mind, it was a wrestling practice, college athletics, two guys fighting according to rules, not hating each other, just fighting according to rules. God, I was powerful. I was a giant. With an endless future ahead of me, a continent of fresh snow.

And I had completely forgotten that trip to the library before seeing Juliana. Good instincts. I don't recall knowing anything at all about women at that age, but apparently I did. Well done. A woman wants to feel that you're interested in her. Even if you aren't truly interested, even if you're interested in her only for your own gratification, to satisfy your own miserable needs, she must feel that you're interested in her. Know what you need, and know how to get it. I may have been confused and annoyed by my need, but I knew what it was, and I was attending to it with good instincts. Well done.

Still, I can't exactly brag. If I had that kind of energy now, that body, knowing what I know now, I could do anything. That kid, he squandered his good looks. He wasted his force, his raw sexual power. I should have had women swooning at my feet. Any young woman I wanted, not the starstruck high school teenyboppers or the ugly ducks who would waddle into the backseat with anybody or the self-righteous Lisas who would make love only to a guy's politics.

Lisa. I can only vaguely remember her now. Who did she think she was? I admit what is obvious: I did not burn my draft card. I did not join the extreme Students for a Democratic Society (who demolished part of the ROTC building my junior year). I did not abandon college to enlist with the Black Panthers. And I am not going to feel bad about it. Certainly I did not approve of the Vietnam War or the inequality of the races or the myriad other social injustices. I certainly did not. I had my ideals. But I was not going to jump on a bandwagon because everybody else did it.

A lot of that stuff was fad, what was fashionable at the time. Look at the guys who were burning their draft cards.

Sensationalists. They wanted attention. They were excited by fire and ash. What did their act accomplish? Some of them were thrown in jail. Many were barred from government employment for life. Or at the least prevented from continuing their education. I would bet that the military establishment didn't suffer one iota from a few elite college guys burning their draft cards. I say: Don't shoot till you see the whites of their eyes. It was a fad, a summer storm that dumped six inches of rain in an hour and moved on.

Yes, I had my ideals, but I was not going to douse myself with gasoline and strike the match, and certainly not for a fad. I was not a follower. Nor, I might add, was Ralph Cunningham, wimpy as he was. At this moment I can hear him talking to someone in the next room. I hear the crack of billiard balls striking each other. Cunningham and some other derelict classmates must be playing pool. They laugh, tap their cue sticks on the floor, rack the balls with a loud thwack. I'm happy that Cunningham has gotten his mind off his obsession for a moment. He needs a rest.

BUT I was arguing about leaders and followers. Take Wayne Manning, my roommate. Wayne may have looked like a concerned citizen and a leader, but Wayne was a goof-off. I remember Wayne. I remember how Wayne used to tape-record the sex whimperings of girls he made love to and later broadcast them out of an open window on football weekends. I remember the night Wayne came home angry because the registrar had refused to let him see his letters of recommendation, and he convinced a bunch of guys to pretend like they had broken into the registrar's file cabinet. They're my fucking records, Wayne said. He tied a string of tuna-fish cans around his waist, dragged them clinking and clattering through campus in the middle of the night, and hoisted a fake file cabinet to the top of the flagpole.

How can you take seriously a goof-off like that? Wayne did what he did for appearance. I don't believe he had any real principles. Wayne threw himself at the Black Panthers the way he threw himself at everything else, a shotgun blast of little Wayne Manning pellets, fired at anything that moved.

Even when Wayne joined the Black Panthers later that year, tossed aside his engineering degree and pissed away his future, I'm sure that he did it for appearance, for some goof-off reason. And where is Wayne now? Where did all of that principled concern get him in life? Wayne Manning has vanished from the face of the earth.

Did I have my own principles? I must have, as naïve and sappy as they were. *I died for Beauty—but was scarce ad-*

justed in the Tomb when One who died for Truth was lain in an adjoining Room. Emily Dickinson. I remember. The grinning gargoyles over the archways. The sound of the rain pecking on the dormer windows of Higinson. The afternoon sun streaming between Davis and Smith, making the tops of the walking posts glitter and break like a row of white waves. Me, beneath a tree with a volume of poetry. The chapel bell chiming the hour. What hour? The hour of everything past. The hour of the branching channels ahead.

EVEN before he enters the aging brick building, he can hear a piano. He listens. Looking up, he sees an open window, three stories over his head. The lilting music descends through the air and blends with the aroma of roast pork and *pastellas* from the bodega on the ground floor. The street seems deserted. An occasional car whisks through, on its way to somewhere else. A woman, wearing a heavy woolen shawl despite the warm air, slumps against the bus-stop post on the corner. Again he checks the address. Against the front of the building, almost hidden by a hanging grocery list for the bodega, a small sign reads: "Morla Magay Dance Studio." He begins climbing the stone stairs, his blood pounding in his ears. *My heart ran so to thee, It would not wait for me.*

REUNION

On the second floor elderly men and women sit in the landing, bored and needy, as if waiting for food stamps. He must step over someone to mount the next flight of stairs. "Morla Magay?" he inquires. A woman shrugs, then points up. Guided by the volume of the piano, he proceeds.

The studio is an ocean of light and air, with a twenty-foot-high ceiling and towering windows facing the street. Mirrors on two walls, peeling paint on another. He sees her immediately. She is in motion. With three other ballerinas, she dances across the room. Their feet on the wood floor sound like a sail ruffling in wind.

"Have a seat," says a woman wearing a leotard and gym shorts. A half-dozen dancers sprawl on the floor and watch the rehearsal in silence. Others exercise quietly in the corners, contorting their bodies into impossible positions. One guy bends a leg behind his back all the way up to his shoulder and grasps his toes with his hand, another man stands on his head against the wall. The room smells of perspiration and perfume.

"Girls," says the director. The piano stops. The director is a bald-headed man with a short cigarette. "You have fingers. Your hands are not plates. You are talking with your body. Now let's go." The director claps his hands to the beat. Clap, clap, clap. One, two, three. "Head back, Miss Lydia." He demonstrates, amazingly graceful for a man in his fifties. With eyes closed, the tiny stump of a cigarette in his mouth, he takes three little steps, his arms swaying behind him like water plants rippling in a stream. Everyone watches the master with total attention. "Now let's go. From the 'Cecchetti.'" The pianist looks up from his paperback novel, which he keeps beside the sheet music, and begins playing again. Bodies become geometry in motion.

She has not seen him. She seems to see nothing while she dances.

By contrast, he cannot take his eyes from her. She is the most fluid of the four. Standing on the toes of one foot, her free leg rises and points to the side like an arrow, one arm drapes behind while another flows upward in a single line. She is a mixture of angles and curves. Seconds later she has transformed herself into a different shape. One leg bends at the knee and crosses her standing leg, her arms form a circular embrace. How he wishes he could stand within that embrace. Now her feet lie flat on the floor, her legs bend slightly at the knee, her arms go down, then she is up on her toes again. She comes down, coils like a spring, jumps into the air, and lands noiselessly with the heel of one foot touching the toes of the other.

The four ballerinas move across the floor like a fluttering of wings, back and forth, around and around, changing shape again and again. At times they become a sequence of

snowflakes. At times they are caged birds, beating for freedom. Angles and curves. Solids and lace. Filigrees of light
trickling through trees. His heart cannot hold all the images and sounds. After a few minutes the ballerinas are
breathing as if there is no oxygen left in the room.

At the break she comes to him, flushed in her face
and her neck. She smiles. "So, you found me." She takes a
long drink from a thermos. "This week I'm one of the
corps," she says between heavy breaths. "Next week I'll be
Odette. She's the queen of the swans." She takes another
drink and dabs her face with a tissue. "Did you like watching me?"

He can hardly express how he feels. "You dance . . ."
Everything he learned in the library he has forgotten.

"I'm going to lose a pound before next week." She
turns and looks at herself in the nearest mirror. "I'm getting down to 104 for Odette."

One of the dancers, an emaciated young woman with
huge blue eyes and chalky white cheeks, walks over with a
noticeable limp and introduces herself. Her name is Lynn,
and she speaks with a British accent. "I missed class this
morning," she says to Juliana. "And do I ever feel it. My
tendons are on fire. Tony knows I missed. He can tell. Did
you see him wag his finger at me?"

"Tony won't do anything unless you miss two in a row,"

says Juliana. "I've got some BZ for your tendons. You can have one if you want. I took two this morning."

"Are you mad? The last time I used BZ, my period stopped for four months. You're going to murder yourself." Lynn bends down and strokes the skinny dog at her feet, then eats a carrot stick and gives one to her dog. "It's bloody hot, I'm sweating away. Two months from now they'll freeze our arses off. Oh, well. Did you hear? Alex is partnering me in *Les Patineurs*."

"She's weirdly jealous of me," Juliana says after Lynn leaves to do knee bends at the horizontal barre. "Alex usually dances with me. Alex actually prefers dancing with me. She'll make a pass at you the next time you come. But we're friends."

Juliana kneels on the floor and takes off her shoes. Her feet are a swollen mass of calluses and blisters. She begins pounding the toe of one shoe against the floor. "Cuts down on the thuds," she says and hands him the other shoe. It is weightless, like her, except for its rock-hard toe.

He holds the shoe and feels that he is holding her. The imagined caress must show on his face. For a moment she looks into his eyes. Does she know what he's thinking? She resumes pounding. "My shoes are the only place I touch the earth," she says. "I want to be light, light, light. Think good thoughts while you work on them."

REUNION

———

CAREFULLY he hits the toe of the shoe against the floor. "You're being too gentle," she says, and laughs. "The shoe can take it." He strikes harder. "That's it," she says.

"What are you rehearsing?" he asks.

She pouts. "Didn't we look like swans? We're doing a trimmed-down Act II of *Swan Lake*. Also, a scene from *Les Patineurs* and a new ballet called *The Drive-In* by some American choreographer."

"You did look like a swan. In a swan world. Do you try to imagine that you're a swan when you dance? What do you think about when you're dancing?"

She pauses to massage her feet. "When I was a little girl, they told me to pretend that I was balancing a champagne glass on my heel. Or moving with my head held by a string from the roof. Now I imagine that a beam of light is coming down on the floor where I am."

"I don't think about anything when I'm wrestling," he says.

"You're a wrestler? I thought so. You've got strong arms." She pushes the toe against the palm of her hand to test how much it has softened.

Strong arms? So she's noticed. He can hardly believe that her eyes have rested upon him. He can hardly believe that he's only inches from her. How old is she? Twenty? Twenty-one? She wears a sleeveless blue shirt, tights, and leg warmers. Her eyes are green and piercing. They appear to be heavily outlined with dark makeup of some kind. He has never seen such eye makeup on anyone except a stage actress, and never so close by. Other than the intensity of her eyes, her face is angelic, her skin smooth and pale. The light from the street window glows in her hair, catches the white curve of her neck, and, falling, illuminates the soft freckles on her shoulders. Her arms and hands have the delicacy of a spring leaf. Legs slender but strong, with visible muscles in her calves. Altogether a goddess, but smaller than she appeared while dancing.

She seems to be still pondering his question. "I guess I don't think about anything either. I listen to the music. I feel my body. Dancing is all I want. I want everyone to see me dance. I want to be as good as Suzanne Farrell. I want to dance with Balanchine. And I will."

Who are Suzanne Farrell and Balanchine? He won't make a fool of himself by asking.

One of the dancers walks by with a garden watering can, sprinkling the wood floor. "It's shit when you slip," she says. "I need to work on the bottoms of my shoes. Will you help me?"

From her bag she produces a penknife and begins scraping the sole of one shoe. Again she hands the other shoe to him. He doesn't have a knife. She tells him to use a key, anything that will rough up the shoes and give them more traction.

"No, don't scrape like that," she says and takes the key from him. She demonstrates what she wants. "Like this." She watches him and nods approval. "Do you wrestle at your college?"

"Yes." Something about her tone embarrasses him. Does she think he is not serious like her because he spends his time in college?

"I'll never go to college," she says. "Even if I had the money. I just want to dance. I started dancing when I was seven. I didn't have a father." While talking, she pauses to study the bottom of her shoe, as if it were a book she was reading. "When I was twelve, I ran away from home and moved in with my aunt, here in the city. She was a dancer when she was young. Ballet, ballet, ballet. At sixteen I joined Magay. My first year I saw Suzanne Farrell dance Dulcinea in *Don Quixote*. I hated her. She was perfect. I am going to dance like that. Dancing is the only perfect thing in the world."

"Emily Dickinson's poetry is perfect," he says.

"I think dancing is poetry too."

He is beginning to understand that dance is not something Juliana does the way he's ever done anything. And this crumbling brick building is not a place where she comes for a few hours a day to get exercise or to perform. This is a temple. And she a priestess, or goddess. How pitiful his life suddenly seems compared to hers. Her life is so simple, focused on one single thing. His mind is filled with uncertainty, hers seems to be certain. He tries to make beauty with words, she creates beauty with her body.

"My blisters are killing me," she says. She takes a needle and black thread from her bag. "Please don't look."

"What are you doing?" he asks.

"Don't look."

"I want to know everything about you." And he realizes that he does. He wants to know where she lives, what movies she watches, what clothes she has in her closet, what she eats for breakfast, who her boyfriends have been. He wants to occupy her, he wants to inject himself into her bloodstream. He doesn't know whether he most desires to make love to her, or to worship her, or both.

One by one she lances each blister, runs the needle and thread through, and leaves the thread in the blister. "I told you not to look," she says. With the black threads hanging from her feet, wet and bloody, she puts her shoes on, stands, and hobbles to the horizontal barre.

"Will you stay for the second half of the rehearsal?" she

calls to him. Without waiting for a reply, she turns and begins knee bends.

How can she dance with her feet in that condition? But
she does, without letting the slightest pain show in her face.
She runs, she leaps, she turns on those feet. He spends the
rest of the afternoon watching her dance, but now he
winces each time her feet touch the floor.

Juliana and the three other swans practice a new series
of steps. Then one of the ballerinas does a duet with a male
dancer, a dark-complexioned man with expressive arms
and massive thigh muscles. He floats with each jump, but
he has a constant scowl on his face. Apparently he disapproves of something the ballerina has done or not done.
Every now and then the bald-headed director goes out with
a tape measure and chalks up the floor. Clap, clap, clap.
One, two, three. "Boys and girls, you are thinking again. I
see you thinking. Don't think." Clap, clap, clap.

When the rehearsal is over, at five o'clock, she asks him
to go with her to the café where she works in the evenings.
They can have something to eat before her shift.

Six

As he walks with her to the subway, he notices that she never makes an ungraceful move. She is always dancing, even here on the grimy streets of the East Village. He wonders if it strains her to constantly carry her body so perfectly. Even in the subway car she sits as if she barely touches the seat, a thin cushion of air between her and every hard surface in the universe. She is fragile and strong at the same time.

The place where she works is called Frankie's Burger and Pizza Joint, west of Central Park. Mounted above the front entrance, a television plays a Laurel and Hardy movie. They walk in and must duck under a specials card hanging by strings from the ceiling. In phosphorescent orange letters: "The Sumo Burger, Over One Pound of Meat."

"Hi, honey," a waitress says to Juliana. "You working early tonight?"

"Not ever," says Juliana. "Six o'clock."

"Um," says the waitress, a huge woman with a mass of little curls. She stares at Charles. "You got a cutie with you."

Juliana leads him past the swivel chairs at the counter to the back, where they find an empty booth. He is hungry. He hasn't eaten anything since breakfast this morning, a century ago.

"Do you live around here?" he asks.

"Near Port Authority. I live with my aunt."

She excuses herself to the bathroom and returns wearing tight-fitting jeans and a halter top, her waitress uniform. Immediately he is aware that men are staring at her. How can she work in this ordinary place, with ordinary people, serving hamburgers and pizza? He wants to protect her, to shield her.

"We've got time to eat," she says. "Order whatever you like, it's free." She waves to one of the waitresses. "Tamara?"

He orders a turkey sandwich with pickles and french fries. She orders coffee, then takes a banana out of her bag.

"Is that all you're eating for dinner?" he asks.

"Don't worry about me. It's normal."

"Are you sure? You can't live on that."

She throws him a look sharp as nails, and he nods, chagrined, aware that he has stumbled over some line.

"Do you like working here?" He hates it that she works in this restaurant.

"I do what I have to do."

Their food comes. He eats, trying not to watch her. Each bite she puts in her mouth seems a painful concession to a physical existence.

"Recite some poetry," she says, "by that person you mentioned. If you know any by heart."

The words come from his mouth before he can stop them:

Love is like Life—merely longer
Love is like Death, during the Grave
Love is the Fellow of the Resurrection
Scooping up the Dust and chanting "Live"!

She listens with the same total attention that she gives to her ballet master. "That's beautiful," she says. "And sad.

The best poetry is sad, don't you think? It must be wonderful to know poetry like that." She begins pinning her hair up in a bun, like the other waitresses. "I read a Hindu poem about reincarnation. Do you believe in reincarnation?"

"Reincarnation?" He hesitates. He doesn't want to say the wrong thing. "No, I don't think so. I believe we die and that's the end. Or maybe some spirit is left that goes somewhere. How about you?"

"I think it has to be true. I just feel all of these life forces everywhere, and I know that I'm part of them. God wouldn't have created so many souls without letting them be part of each other. I want to come back as my mother, before she got crazy. I want to know her. I just want to know her." She glances at the clock over the counter. "I have to work now. Why don't you stay awhile? You can sit here, no one will bother you. I'll come over and say hello every few minutes."

He stays. He follows her with his eyes as she moves from one table to the next carrying cardboard trays of sandwiches and pizza, into the kitchen and back, to the counter to wipe up spilled soda and beer, to the garbage container with half-eaten hamburgers and dirty napkins. She is too fine for this, he thinks. Even now, balancing a tray of crappy food in this crappy place, she moves like a dancer, she moves like a heavenly being. He wants to take her out of this place.

When she is not within view, he watches the hour hand move slowly around the clock. After four hours he gets up from the table. His bus leaves at eleven.

"I've got to go," he says to her as she comes out of the kitchen.

"Stay," she says. "I get off at midnight."

"The last bus leaves at eleven." How can he possibly stay? He'll miss the last bus back to school. Already he's missed most of the day's classes. And where would he sleep? At her aunt's house? He tries to picture himself sleeping on the sofa of her aunt's house, wherever it is, a cramped dusty room, a grandfather clock ticking through the night.

As she turns to inspect one of her tables, he notices that her order pad has made a red crease in the small of her back. Her eyeliner is smeared. Somewhere a toilet flushes. Suddenly an undefinable thing sweeps over him. Why is he here, in this dingy café in New York City? A few hours ago he believed that he knew why, he believed in this beautiful woman, this place, buildings. Now nothing makes sense. The dance studio and the dancers seem like a distant dream slipping by in the night. Juliana a dream herself, even though she stands in front of him, exhausted and sweating. He is lost. He is a seed of grass in the wind.

All of these thoughts pass through his head in an instant. He cannot think, he is overwhelmed and confused.

"I've got to go," he says awkwardly, unable to find other words. He moves toward the door.

"Come back next week," she says. "I'll be the swan queen."

M Y stomach. My stomach. It's in my throat. I'm shaking.

Oh God. I didn't know I had such feelings for her after all of these years. Yes I did. I want to touch her all over again.

I have thought of her, of course. But seeing her. I can hardly stand up. My legs buckle. I am breathing hard. I can't. Calm down. Calm down. Calm down.

But her eyes, I remember them as blue, not green. Her eyes were blue.

I H A D forgotten that first night. The beginning and the end. Am I going to live through that raw year again? I want to remember: When was the very last time I saw her? I want to remember what she was wearing, the tilt of her shoulders, the last word she said to me. But that was months later. Some of it was beautiful. I cannot think about her. I must think about something else.

I . . . I am ashamed of myself. What a stupid jerk I was. To get that kind of invitation from her and not know what to do with it. I had forgotten that first night.

I would like to say something to my twenty-two-year-old self. Just between the two of us. How does one address his twenty-two-year-old self? Is my twenty-two-year-old self me, or not me?

Now I understand how I should talk to him: You idiot! You fool! How could you not see that she was coming on to you, that she wanted you, that she was offering herself to you! The goddess was asking you to spend the night in heaven with her. Didn't she say: "Stay." That's what I heard. Are you deaf? What do you think "Stay" means? You're twenty-two years old, you're not a child. What do you think it means when a woman says "stay" late at night? You have embarrassed me. You have embarrassed yourself, and you are not even aware of it.

It is astonishing that she invited you to visit again, after you acted like such a jerk. Women do not like to be turned down. You knew nothing about women. How you wasted the moment, wasted your power. You deserve what you got. You deserved to go home alone and confused on that two-hour bus ride in the middle of the night through dim little towns, people wheezing and coughing so that you couldn't doze off for five minutes, the bus stinking with fumes from a broken exhaust pipe. Thinking only of rescuing her from that crummy hamburger joint. Fantasizing that you could swoop down on your white steed and whisk her away.

Those were noble feelings, of course, but ultimately foolish, misplaced angst, wasted energy. Why did you think that you could decide what was best for Juliana? What did you know of her needs? You should have looked after yourself. That is what I want to say to you. It is not only that you knew nothing about women. You knew nothing about yourself.

Am I sounding like a selfish shit again? I am only being honest. At bottom people are selfish. And that primordial selfishness, which our species goes to great pains to deny, seems to underlie most human behavior. Isn't that what Adam Smith was talking about with his "self-interest" as the basis for capitalism? Or Deborah Raeke, in her terrifying novel *The Morning of Artifice*? There. I'm thinking about something else now. I feel better. *The Morning of Artifice*.

The sentence I remember best is: "We are all mothers and daughters of our own anxiety." What is the anxiety? That we cannot accept our selfish natures.

———

IN Raeke's book, which I often assign to my students, two women in their late thirties are brought together after losing their husbands. One man died of an embolism, the other precipitously ran off with his secretary. Finding themselves alone, and having been friends during their married lives, the women move in with each other. Dorothy and Katherine. At the time the novel opens, the two women have been living together in a quiet apartment for many years, each having had fleeting love affairs in the past, now forgotten. Both are gainfully employed, Dorothy as a secretary and Katherine as a dental hygienist. At home Dorothy does the shopping and takes care of the dog and two cats. Katherine cleans house and pays the bills. Dorothy massages Katherine's swollen feet at night while they watch television. They sometimes entertain friends on their third-floor balcony, which has wrought-iron chairs with comfortable cushions and a fine view of the reservoir nearby. During their annual two weeks of summer vacation, always the first two weeks of August, they travel. One year they went to Acapulco, another year to Paris. Their affection for each other has grown through the years. In fact, one rainy evening in their early forties they made love, but then mutually decided that a physical relationship might jeopardize their deep friendship, which was already ripe with its own intimacies.

Two hundred pages into the novel, with the women in their mid-sixties, Dorothy is diagnosed with breast cancer. She is dying. She has endured the usual chemotherapy and radiation treatments, but she cannot be saved. Old friends visit. Her brother visits. As she lies withered in her bed, her hair gone, her voice frail as a reed, Katherine breaks down. "What will happen to me?" she cries out. "Who will drive? Who will get the groceries?"

At first such small-minded and selfish protests seem like a grave misstep of the novelist. What real person could be concerned only for herself at this terrible moment, insensitive to the agonies of her loved one? But then we realize that the relationship with Dorothy has always served Katherine's needs. And vice versa. For years, despite appearances, the two women acted completely out of self-interest. All of the tender words between them, all the mutual kindnesses, the little favors, even the one instance of sexual congress, were in fact completely quid pro quo, gifts designed to repay the giver.

Such an explanation of behavior need not be accompanied by any moral verdict. It is simply the truth. The law of all living things. Katherine, with her selfish outcries, seems to recognize this truth. Or if she does not clearly recognize this truth, at least her primitive unconscious does. Her primitive being knows what it needs.

When I first read Raeke's book, years ago, I was horrified by its implications. Could I have misinterpreted the novel? Was Katherine, overcome by the impending death of her dear friend, simply expressing her love in terms of the small things that they shared? Or was she so out of her mind with grief that she put meaningless words together? I wanted to be wrong. Against my better judgment, I attempted to correspond with the author. But Deborah Raeke, after publishing her single great book, had disappeared. And I am left with my dark theories.

IT is not until several days later, as he walks out of his philosophy class, that he realizes his stupendous failure. Failure not in the obvious sense. What torments him is the thought that he disappointed her. Now, walking across the diagonal path to the gymnasium, he painfully remembers every word that he said and did not say, the awkwardnesses and the silences. He is rotten with women.

During wrestling practice, he cannot concentrate. Instead he broods over his confused feelings about her. What does she really want from him? Why does he feel guilty? Despite the confusion, he believes that he is falling in love.

A whistle blows. His eyes partly focus, and he sees the lunge of his opponent, a fleshy bulk in blue gym shorts. "Headlock," yells the coach. The bodies separate, he stares vaguely at the mass of pink stomach and thinks of her flushed neck, the thin crystal of her skin. Why does he suffer like this? Something from the morning's lecture on existentialism lodges in his brain. *Although the individual cannot live without suffering, anxiety, and guilt, these three experiences exist beyond any rational comprehension.*

"Pin!" the coach shouts, and he realizes that he has been pinned. Surprisingly he feels no defeat. Sweat drips down on his face from the student above him. Light shines in his eyes. He rises to a kneeling position and has the sensation of watching himself move in slow motion, listening to himself think.

What he is thinking: He has learned nothing in college. His books are bricks scratched with the dried words of dead men.

Still moving in slow motion, he walks to the showers. He strips, he inhales the thick clouds of steam. Unbeckoned, the ugly thought occurs to him: How often has she taken men to Frankie's to wait while she finished her shift? He imagines a platoon of eligible males, marching into her restaurant night after night, summoned to wait for her in the vinyl booth. College guys, dancers, young businessmen, lawyers, doctors. In front of the restaurant he stops one of the guys, the lawyer, dressed in an uptown pin-striped suit, a monogrammed collar, a silk tie as wide as a fist, an alligator belt, matching alligator loafers with those pompous tassels. Not Juliana's type at all. The lawyer thinks that she will dust him with a little high culture, a little art, and he in turn will lift her above her miserable station in life and, of course, escort her to his apartment on Fifth Avenue, to his wood-paneled bedroom with his rowing medals from Yale on the wall, his law certificates, the four-poster bed and the pale blue sheets. It is eleven o'clock in the evening. He's going to wait for her in the vinyl booth for one hour, no longer. Where are you going? Charles asks angrily. The lawyer briefly glances at him as if he were a wedge of soggy pizza lying on the sidewalk. You're not going to see Juliana, are you? Charles asks. Who are you? says the lawyer. You look like a college boy. Please get out of my way. The lawyer reaches for the door with his gloved hand. He has that overindulged look. This is all a game to him. He doesn't care about Juliana as such. What gives him his thrill is driving up in his Mercedes to this crummy pizza joint, stepping out on the filthy sidewalk in his tasseled shoes, rubbing shoulders with the neighborhood lowlife, sitting in the cheap vinyl booth, ordering the cheap food. Then playing with the beautiful but unwashed young girl. He'll make her his slave. Tonight he's carrying a box of expensive chocolates for her. So little does he know about Juliana, to believe that she would eat even one quarter of a chocolate candy. What delicious fun, he thinks, bringing Belgian chocolates into this barnyard. He leans down and breathes in the rich smell of the chocolates, a sugary form of everything rich in his life, like his calf-leather briefcase or the skin of the young women after he washes them in his oversize bathtub. Charles punches him hard. The box of chocolates falls to the ground. For a moment the lawyer sags, then rises again to his full height. Charles hits him again. You can't hurt me, college boy, the lawyer says and laughs.

Charles slams his hand into the tiled wall of the shower stall. The jealousy grows hard in his mind and turns into a hard grinning knot that sinks in his stomach. Jealousy. Add that to the list of existential incomprehensibles.

IN the dining hall that night, he hears on the radio that the Vietcong have been using Cambodian territory for attacks against South Vietnam. The announcement brings an uproar at his table.

"Tomorrow morning we'll be bombing Cambodia," someone shouts.

"I have a brother in Vietnam," says another student, "and he says that we've been bombing Cambodia for years. Eastern Cambodia."

"No shit."

"He saw a whole family burned to charcoal. Sleeping in their hut."

"Who do those assholes think they are?"

"That's your fine government, weenie. They're little boys playing with their toys."

"Johnson should be put in jail as a war criminal. We're in because of LBJ."

"Johnson's never fired his own dick."

Charles closes his eyes and tries to picture himself in Vietnam. How can people he doesn't know, people he's never seen before, force him to go to Vietnam? Nothing is real.

"What do you have to say, Major Blanchard? Are you working Cambodia?" Someone is taunting Nick Blanchard, who has not bothered to take off his ROTC uniform before dinner.

"I'll work wherever they send me," says Nick, with a smirk on his face. "I'm just a whore."

Nick gets up from his chair and sits next to Charles and Ralph. "Every time they do something stupid, I take the shit for it," he says in a low voice.

"You spoke well," says Charles. "You said what you had to. Davis is an asshole."

"Listen," says Nick. "How would you gentlemen like to go shooting with me on a farm up near Topsfield this weekend?"

Somehow Nick has gotten hold of three semiautomatic twenty-two rifles from last summer's ROTC training camp. Not something he's publicizing, but he's anxious to try them out. Charles wants no part of it.

"Rabbits, that's all we'll be shooting," says Nick in his silky-soft voice. "The lady on the farm said we'd be doing her a favor to kill a few rabbits. They're eating her gardens."

"I don't know anything about guns," says Ralph.

"There's nothing to it," says Nick. "I can teach you in ten minutes. They make a big stink about shooting rifles in training, but that's just part of their brainwashing routine. There's nothing to it."

"I don't want to go," Ralph says, primping his crew cut. "I'm not into poaching and maiming. Anyway, I've got reading to do before Monday."

"The farm is beautiful," says Nick. "There's acres of

fields and a lake. You've never seen such a peaceful lake, like a postcard. It's got tons of black-spotted trout. The rabbits are beautiful too. And they're fast, so there's some challenge to it. The lady said we could take any rabbits we killed. I figure we're doing a good deed."

"You go with Charles," says Ralph. "Bring me back a rabbit. I'll do something with it. I'll have it stuffed."

"What do you say, Charlie?" says Nick.

"I'd like to go to the lake," says Charles. "But not to destroy stuff."

"Fuck you guys," says Nick.

Charles is thinking that Nick probably doesn't care one iota about shooting rabbits, that he just wants to handle some unauthorized military hardware. And he's doing it secretly, the hidden insult as always. Still, there's something about Nick that Charles admires.

SEVEN

ON Sunday the three boys drive up to the farm in Nick's 1955 Chevrolet. It seems like the first day of autumn, with quick stabs of orange and red in the trees, tall grasses on the side of the road, a clarity in the air from the night's sudden dew.

Charles is glad to be out in the country for a day. He leans out of the window and breathes in the vast openness. Years ago he went on a camping trip with his father, canoeing and fishing, and the memory remains bright in his mind. It was just that once, but he thinks of it now and feels that here he is in the bosom of another family of sorts: Nick behind the steering wheel, smoking his special Turkish cigarettes, Ralph in the backseat studying the compass he has bought for the occasion.

A half hour into the drive, Nick makes it known that his parents want him to quit ROTC. Evidently they read in *The Pig* about the two ROTC students who were beaten up by fellow classmates. "They don't understand that we'll have to pay back all the money, which we don't have," Nick says, tossing a cigarette stub out the window. "My father's got this crap job that earns fourteen thousand dollars a year, can't pay for shit, and he's telling me what to do. No way, José. I'm twenty-one. I can do what I want. The ROTC is paying my way."

"Right on, sister," says Ralph from the backseat. "People got to do what they got to do. I wouldn't put on that fascist uniform myself for a thousand bucks, but I'm not you."

"Up yours," says Nick. "You'd put on my uniform if it fit." Nick makes the car swerve back and forth a couple of times on the empty road and grins in the rearview mirror. "My parents are calling me three times a week. Do this, do that, get your ass home. Can you believe it? Do your parents tell you what to do?"

"My parents don't care what I do," says Ralph. "They're soused most of the time, anyway. All they care about is going to parties at their lily-white club and hanging out with high society. We get along."

"Hooboy."

"My parents want me to be an engineer," says Charles, "like my father. They're pissed that I haven't taken one engineering class, but they don't tell me they're pissed. They just talk about all of my high school friends and what they're studying in college and the great jobs they're getting. I wouldn't do what my father does for a million dollars."

"What does he do?" asks Ralph.

"He works for Dow Chemical. He improves the way that they make calcium chloride pellets." In his mind Charles sees his father coming into the kitchen after work, powdery lime dust on his pants legs, proud of the white dust.

"I might do that," says Ralph.

"I'm sick and tired of getting called three times a week, like I was in kindergarten," says Nick. "What's the worst that could happen? I could get beat up."

"You're not going to get beat up," says Charles. "Tell your parents you're not going to get beat up. And if you do get beat up, it probably won't be because you're in ROTC. People get beat up for no reason. If I were your parents, I'd be worried about what happens to you after you graduate. When you go to Vietnam."

"There's not a snowball's chance in hell I'm going to Vietnam," says Nick.

"Spoken like a true soldier," says Ralph.

For the next twenty minutes they ride in silence. Then, after a shabby, one-pump Esso gas station, they turn off the highway. The last two miles are a winding dirt road with a barbed-wire fence on both sides.

They park the car next to a peeling white mailbox and begin walking. In the distance, cornfields stretch out as far as the eye can see, browning but still standing tall. Nick and Ralph are carrying the rifles, Charles the boxes of cartridges. When they get to an empty barn, Nick shows the novices how to load the magazine, hold the rifle butt in the crook of the shoulder, aim, and squeeze the trigger as if it were soft butter. They practice shooting a few rounds into a tree stump. The rifles make sharp cracks as they're fired.

"I told you it was easy," says Nick. "You can hit the rabbit anywhere and you'll kill it. These are twenty-two longs. Yes sir. One of these could kill a man. It's good to know how to use a gun. You might have to protect yourself someday, you never know. I'm planning on keeping a pistol on me at all times."

"Yes sir," says Ralph.

They follow the dirt path around the side of the barn and out toward the fields. As they walk single file, the land rises above them, moist and full. Pale patches of trees on the horizon. Smell of honeysuckle.

"We're heading 273 degrees," says Ralph.

"What difference does it make where we're heading," Charles says. "Captain Blanchard knows the way."

"I don't see any rabbits."

"The rabbits don't come here, weenie," says Nick. "The gardens are over there," and he points to a misty spot in the distance.

Now they're a mile from the car. They walk in silence. Geese fly overhead, honking and ruffling, and the blue-green grasses gently sway on the high ground, and there is a low buzz in the air from the aggregation of millions of un-seen animals, all alive and crawling and making their mi-nute sounds of life. Charles is enjoying himself. It seems to him that they are all enjoying themselves. Where is Juliana now? he wonders. He imagines her in her aunt's Sunday apartment. She sits on a velvet sofa, brushing her aunt's vel-vety hair. When she looks up and smiles at him, there is no mistaking the smile. She loves him as he loves her. Velvety, velutinous, voluptuous. Please love me back. Please. I will consecrate myself to you. To his right, a sudden sound: a fox darts by in the brush, the white tip of a tail. He is walking on the trail, single file, the middle man.

Then they reach the gardens, haphazard rows of tomatoes, lettuce and cabbage, beans, a wooden toolshed. Rabbits are hopping everywhere. Ralph raises his rifle to shoot.

"Not now," whispers Nick. "As soon as you shoot, you scare them away. We all need to start shooting at the same time, that way we get the most shots in. We'll get five, maybe six shots each."

In order to triangulate the nearest garden, Nick positions Charles and Ralph fifty feet apart. He's going to station himself off to the side, in the toolshed, and give the order to fire. So far the rabbits are casually moving about, oblivious to the hunters. "Aren't they something," Nick whispers with excitement. "I'm glad you guys came. I told you you'd like it."

Charles stands in his spot, aiming at one of the rabbits, waiting for Nick's signal to shoot. Now the juice is pumping hard through his body. There is something thrilling about hunting game, thrilling and terrible at the same time. His rabbit, fifty feet away, has thick brownish-gray fur. He can see its bright eyes, its huge feet like house slippers. But his hands are shaking. Before today he's never held a real rifle. He looks at Ralph, who is bent over his own rifle in concentration. Maybe Ralph is nervous too. Charles thinks again about Juliana brushing her aunt's hair, and he is thinking that she would probably detest what he's doing now, that she wouldn't understand why he's doing it. Then he thinks about his father, and how his father taught him to wrestle at a young age, taught him how to grab a guy suddenly and startle him and how to inflict a little pain, even if you didn't need to, because it showed the other guy that you were not afraid to get hurt yourself and it helped demoralize him.

Suddenly the rabbits sense danger. They start to run.

"Shoot," yells Nick. Nick's rifle cracks. Immediately Ralph throws down his rifle without firing a shot and sits on the ground. Charles sees him out of the corner of his eye, fires his first shot, misses. He fires again. It is just him and Nick shooting. He sights wildly on another rabbit, a blur of beautiful speed, and pulls the trigger. Where's Nick? The guns are cracking now, one crack after another. A rabbit screams. Rabbits zigzag madly in all directions, into the surrounding fields. The rabbits are so swift and beautiful, Charles cannot help but stare at them even though he's shooting. There are dozens of them, maybe hundreds, they seem to be coming out of the ground, their bellies flash white and gray and brown, they make quick furry arcs as they hop and bound on their big feet, their ears spread wide like wings, and they fill the air with an odd shuffling noise. Another scream. Two rabbits lie motionless. Crack. Crack, the sound is sharp like a whip. A falling spent shell brushes his arm and burns.

In seconds the rabbits have vanished. A cloud of smoke drifts silently through the garden. Still sitting on the ground, Ralph begins singing some ridiculous song, *Did you see her do "The Mississippi Waltz"?* Charles's head pounds with the recent cracks of the rifles, and his mouth feels dry.

After a few moments Nick comes out of the toolshed, and together they walk to the two dead rabbits. One is split open, and its entrails lie next to it. The other looks completely untouched, as if it were only asleep, its head tucked under one furry ear. Nick bends down and studies the two rabbits but doesn't touch them. The expression on his face is strange, one Charles has never seen before. "There's a third," he says, rising. Another rabbit lies twenty feet away, behind a row of cabbages, twitching and trying to get up. "That's yours," Nick says in his silky voice. "You've got some shots left. Finish him off."

Charles walks to the wounded rabbit, stands over it. "I can't," he says.

"You've got to finish him off," says Nick. "It's not right to leave him like that."

Charles looks down at the shuddering rabbit. His stomach heaves. "You and your goddamned military stuff. I wish we hadn't come here." For the first time he realizes how much he hates Nick.

Nick unlatches the safety on his rifle and shoots the rabbit in the head. Charles can see Nick's hands shaking. Nick shoots a second time. Then he drops his rifle and hides his face. He takes a step back, stumbles slightly, and sways. After a few moments he says in a muffled voice: "Let's get out of here. Okay?"

Charles says nothing.

"I want to go. Can we go?"

Charles turns and for the first time sees the lake, a shimmering blue pearl in the distance.

AFTER the hunting trip, every loud noise makes Charles cringe. There are days when he cannot bear even the shouts of other students in the hallways, or the slam of a door. Solitude and quiet, that is what he wants. And Juliana.

In the evenings he studies at his little desk in the library, three stories below ground. There he has found silence. From time to time, fragments of hushed voices escape through the shelves, scholastic discussions, personal confessions magnified by the mazelike acoustics and the musty odor of old books in the narrow, sleeping aisles. Then the midnight walk home: the damp autumn air, the lampposts casting their sudden pencil-like shadows.

Again he has been counting the hours until he can see her. And he has completed his poem to her. *An hour of eternity, a moment in your eyes* . . . He will take her, as well, a volume of Emily Dickinson. He will enjoy giving her gifts.

Late Thursday night, the day before he is going to visit her, he returns to his room and finds a message: He shouldn't come to New York. She will call again in a few days. He is frantic. After a sleepless night he telephones her dance studio. An irritable woman answers and says that rehearsal does not begin until noon. Juliana dances there from noon until five every day of the week. Call again at noon. Where is she now? he asks. She's taking class, on St. Mark's Place, from nine-thirty to eleven every day of the week. But the classroom has no telephone. He strains to remember the aunt's name.

After his Modern European History class, he stops at the student center and calls the studio again. Yes, she is there, but a rehearsal is in session and she cannot be interrupted.

That night he reaches her at Frankie's. She is sweet on the telephone but anxious and vague. She has been ill, she says. This is a bad place to call her, she can't talk more than a minute, she'll call him tomorrow or the next day. When? he asks. He'll wait by the telephone. She can't talk now, she says. She'll call him. She hangs up, and he feels that the blood has been let out of him.

Briefly he considers the idea of going uninvited to her studio. If he could see her face, even for a second, perhaps he would know whether she cares about him. But the idea evaporates in self-doubt. He has endured too many rejections by women to open himself up for another. She is a tease after all.

In the following days he loses interest in his classes. The familiar emptiness. His books lie heavy and unopened on the painted desk by his bed. Most days he sleeps away like a drunk. He must get over her. This too has happened before.

Then, a week later, she calls in the middle of the night, waking up all of his roommates. Will he come to the studio tomorrow to see her rehearsing? Yes, he says immediately. She has missed him, she says. Before he can think, she has hung up.

EIGHT

THE next day it rains. He leaves campus on the noon bus to New York and arrives at the Morla Magay studio at half past two. Despite the weather, he has not worn a raincoat, as if to increase his misery, and is drenched. When he enters the studio, Juliana is dancing a pas de deux. Tony, puffing his short stub of a cigarette, leans against an iron radiator and claps to the music. Tchaikovsky. Can he close his eyes and just listen? Can he forget himself for a few minutes?

From across the room, Lynn spots him and glides past the pianist. "Can't stay away from her," she whispers, and smiles. "Or did you come to see me?" She stands very close to him, so close that he can see a vein throbbing in her neck.

"I heard Juliana's been sick," he says. "Is she feeling better?"

"Is that what she said?" says Lynn. "We're all sick. Starving and sick. We kill ourselves for it. I'd weigh ten pounds more if I weren't dancing." Ten pounds wouldn't be nearly enough, he thinks. He can count her ribs one by one through her leotard. "Juliana tells me you're a wrestler."

They watch Juliana and her partner spin and float around the room. If Juliana has been ill, there are no signs of it now. She holds the swanlike positions without effort and shapes them in an unfolding line. Her partner rushes at her, she retreats coyly. The prince and the swan queen look ecstatically in love, and they convey their love completely through facial expressions and movement. He finds that he is jealous of the male dancer, envious of each glance, each touch of Juliana's hands and her waist. He can barely look.

"What do you think?" says Lynn.

"A dream," he says.

"Juliana works very hard." Lynn does some stretches in front of him, but when he pays no attention to her, she walks away. For a moment he thinks that he should walk away as well, leave this studio and never come back, return to . . . what?

When the rehearsal is over, he gives Juliana the book of

poetry, and she seems pleased. She asks him to go with her to Frankie's. "Why?" he says, holding the door for her. "Why should I go to Frankie's with you?" He is mystified by her, hurt, in love all at the same time.

"Do I have to explain it?" she says softly. "Just come with me."

"Why did you cancel last time? The night before?"

"Please stop asking me questions. I like being with you." She slips her hand in his, and he melts.

At midnight, after her waitressing shift is over, she takes him back to the studio. They climb the three flights of stairs in silence, he following behind her, their feet falling in soft taps on the stone steps. She has a key. In the dark they walk through the studio, past the shadowy shape of the piano, to the rear, and out into a narrow corridor. Not until they reach the small door of the women's dressing room does she turn on a light. The ballerinas have turned their over-size closet into an encampment. Lipsticks, mascara, bobby pins, combs and brushes, hair sprays and tissues, curling irons, colored cosmetic pencils, dried flowers litter the counter beneath the large oblong mirror. The slightest draft would blow away the photographs of boyfriends tacked to the low ceiling. But there is no moving air in this inner room of an inner room.

She closes the door and hangs her bag on a clothes rack

laden with costumes and lacy brassieres. It is so quiet that they can hear the ticking of the clock in the studio down the hall. Then she turns and kisses him.

Embracing her, he notices for the first time the little beauty mark on her lip. Even her slight imperfections make her more perfect. He studies her face, trying to fathom her.

Without speaking, she undresses herself, slowly, then him. She has firm, perfect little breasts, just as he has imagined. He feels himself trembling, and she holds him. Holds him against her smooth skin. They make love leaning against the wall. Her body is fragile, supple, perfect. He thinks that she was made for him. At first she shows him just how she wants him to touch her. Then he devours her. His hunger is huge, as if he's been starved for a lifetime. He devours her, her arms and legs glowing and long in the night, the long sweep of her, fragrant and holy. Her ocean pours through him, he drowns in her, he wants all of her, drinks all of her piercing and sweet. He drowns and is glad in his drowning. Somewhere she moves against him, noiselessly, as if she were dancing, except at her climax when she cries out. The cry rushes and bursts and reverberates in his ears. His own release is so strong, so impossible, that from its pinnacle he falls into a deep oblivion. When he regains consciousness, he is still folded into her, against the wall. And she is looking at her body in the mirror.

———

JUST before dawn she leaves him to go back to her aunt's apartment. "I have to put in an appearance," she says, dressing hurriedly. She tells him that she wants him to stay for her morning class, just another few hours, then he can return to his college. He will do anything she asks. She scribbles the address on a crumpled piece of paper, kisses him, and is gone. Shuddering, he listens to her feet on the studio floor, the soft closing of the front door.

He naps and reads magazines and takes the subway to St. Mark's Place, where she has class. When she arrives, she kisses him quickly on the lips, then begins her warm-up stretches. Everyone starts at the barre. The dancers wear all manner of odd clothing: leotards paired with iridescent gym shorts, cut-off tights and kneesocks, leg warmers, sweatshirts and T-shirts, ribbons streaming from ballet slippers, billowing unbuttoned white shirts, snug hats and headbands. Yet the atmosphere is dead serious. No one jokes, no one talks. Each dancer silently concentrates on his or her own body. The dancers are beautiful race cars, and this is the shop, the oiling and tuning and fine adjustment of gears.

"Plié," says the teacher, a middle-aged woman with a ferocious countenance. The teacher strides back and forth down the rows of dancers at the barres, snapping her fingers to the music. "Tendu." Legs stretch to the sides. She motions what she wants with her arms: "Two front, two side, two inside." Everyone moves in unison, like a military regiment.

Miraculously, he catches her eye, and she smiles. She must love him.

"Rond de jambe," barks the teacher. Legs sketch little circles in the air. "Fondue." This pianist seems to possess a sense of humor and begins to play "Ragtime" to get the blood flowing and lighten the fierce ambition in the air.

Later the dancers move to the center of the room and begin with pirouettes. "Fondue, extend, second, rond de jambe, plié, pas de bourrée, tendu, plié, fourth, pirouette." He is a traveler to a foreign country.

He feels himself falling. He wants to spend every minute with her, he wants to possess her, her purity, her body, her mind. She is what he has been waiting for. Now he can live. As if for the first time, he looks out and sees. Paintings. Air. Space. Sunlight flows through the large double window and glows in successive cascades on the petals of the hanging geraniums, the brass horizontal barre, the scuffed wooden floor. Perhaps in love we can understand something of human experience, he thinks. Poetry and love.

On the bus back to school, he hardly notices the sharp

edge of the seat, the stopping and starting at each little town. Instead moments of their night together burn like hot stars in his mind. Her look of delight as she read his poem, and then read it again. The way that she buried her head in his shoulder and gripped his hand. The pained pleasure on her face as he pleased her. Her crashing cry out. All gifts that he holds in his heart. He wishes to give to her again and again. Her smell is all over his body.

Her fragrance, yes, I think I can still smell it after all of these years. After all of these years, I am still overcome, I can't hold myself back. Odd, the way a smell has more staying power than all other senses, or words. There I was, enduring that interminable bus trip that I was to take so many times, her smell on my legs and my chest. Of course I remember her fragrance. Perspiration mixed with perfume, was it? But for Juliana, even her perspiration was delicate, it drove me so insane with desire that I would sometimes lick the sweat from her body. Especially the hollow between her breasts. Her skin exuded a natural lavender bouquet, as if she had just bathed in a field of those pale blue flowers. How could I not remember.

And that ballerinas' dressing room. I have opened its small door so many times in the last thirty years. The long mirror, the tiny glass bottles that tinkled and clattered, the mauve silk scarf strung across the ceiling. But the costume rack was not in the dressing room. It was outside in the corridor. Not a clothes rack, really, but a row of wooden pegs in the wall. We would take the costumes into the dressing room and put them on the floor to lie down on, our tinsel bed, our only bed for those months. And the door, made of painted plywood, hardly able to muffle the sexual detonations that came from that little room.

What a night, that first night with Juliana, the first night of my life. A universe awaited me. I was a universe myself. How gorgeously reckless I was. With such grand foolishness I wasted the hours. Six hours waiting for her in the vinyl booth at Frankie's, another four sitting alone on the makeup counter in the ballerinas' dressing room while she showered at her aunt's house. The hours meant nothing. I would have gladly wasted many more hours. For what does time matter in the extravagance of youth? When an infinity of hours and years stretches in front of you, what do a few hours here or there matter? I was immortal.

I was immortal. I am sickened with envy. I could kick that young kid. When I gaze upon myself at twenty-two years old, see the unwrinkled skin, the taut body, the clear eyes, the raw power and passion . . . the world waited for me, and I was as unconcerned as if an uncle had given me a small gift for my birthday. "Thank you, Uncle, for that little obligatory gift. I am not completely ungrateful. But next time I may not thank you at all because I deserve a thousand gifts larger than that. A thousand birthdays wait over the curve of the earth, and what is one small present, more or less? I am sorry, but I cannot be concerned." That was my attitude. How glorious, how decadent. Let the world wait. It makes me nauseous.

O F course, anyone would be sick with envy, and I am going on too long, but I do wish to make one point. Young people explode with their discovery of the world and the newness of life. They sleep and sleep in their tiny cocoons, and suddenly one day, perhaps in one moment, as in the moment Juliana first kissed me, suddenly a young person wakes up and finds the universe tilting and gasping in front of him. Infinity. So many things are happening for the first time. What young people don't realize is that so much is happening for the last time as well. The world is both opening and closing at once.

The first kiss, the first ecstasy of love, the play of light in the trees on a particular fall day, the endless flood of strength in our biceps and thighs. We have the illusion that all of this will happen again and again. In a way this falseness of youth is even more painful than the branching channels ahead. For the young are very much aware of the moment of the first kiss, the first ecstasy of love, and so on. They are keenly aware. Their terrible miscalculation is thinking that these moments will repeat in the infinity of time, that their bodies and minds will hold.

Do I sound like a pedant? I say *we* and I say *young people,* but I really mean *me.* I was a young person. I thought that these moments would repeat and repeat in the infinity of time. I thought that my mind and my boy's body would hold. I thought that I would see Juliana dance week after week, year after year. I believed that I could hold her body against mine whenever I wished, talk to her always about dancing and poetry, forever watch as she gingerly shaved her legs in the sink of the dressing room, the pink curve of her slowly coming out of the white. I thought that she loved me and would love me forever.

Although I was prepared to suffer, it never occurred to me that she might be using me the way that Lena used Ulrich. It never occurred to me that she might need me, and other men, merely for a liberation that ballet could not bring. Those thousands of pirouettes and pliés, perhaps they were more rigid than they seemed, perhaps they denied her some kind of total physical experience, so that what she still needed badly, or at least what her body understood that it still needed badly, was a string of gigantic orgasms. It never occurred to me that she might travel from one man to the next to avoid being abandoned. Or to avoid being worshiped like a goddess, a worship she both relished and despised.

The irony is that she became a ballerina in order to gain some control over her body when she could control nothing else in her life. She . . . but I am only guessing. I didn't understand her then, and I don't understand her now. In many ways she was like my wife, whom I also never understood. Barbara also came from a broken family, also was intensely committed to a profession, in her case the law. She was always far more ambitious than I and tenderly resented me for it, never quite saying that I should have positioned myself for a faculty job at one of the big Ivy League universities, never quite saying that I should have written books instead of reading them, that she preferred not to find me in my robe and slippers when she came home at seven o'clock wanting me to rub her neck. She resented that she made much more money than I did. Barbara came from a family that had nothing, dairy farmers in Pennsylvania, and she should have been overjoyed at her big salary, the law review, the prestigious firm, her set of accomplished friends. And yet, mysteriously, she wanted me to provide the security. No. I wouldn't do it. I was happy with her success, I constantly congratulated her, but I was not going to ruin my life trying to exceed her success, especially for some illusive and irrational reason. She did love me. I give her that. She wept when I got lost on a walking tour in Yosemite Park. She wept when Emily and I fought. She wept when I told her that I couldn't live with her anymore. Then, when we split up, she left me everything, knowing I would take it. Rubbed her success in my face.

And I have forgotten the point I was making. What was I saying? I was talking about Juliana. Sometimes I would arrive at the Magay studio between sessions and find her and Lynn stretched out on the floor with their long legs, paging through one of the fashion magazines. A century ago. "I wouldn't waste my time on him," Juliana would say, pointing at one of the models and sipping from her thermos. "Men like that don't notice you." Lynn would whisper something, and they would start giggling like schoolgirls, and then hide the magazine under a sweatshirt as soon as they saw me. I remember that sometimes Juliana would hum a church song, very softly, just for herself. She had been in a church choir when she was a little girl, one of the few things she told me about her childhood. A Methodist church, I think it was. Her singing voice was clear and pure and lilting, and I think it brought her some kind of comfort. If I ever asked her to sing louder, she would realize that I had been listening and stop altogether. Juliana had a certain sweet shyness mixed with her ambition and drive.

Her singing was the one thing her mother would ask about when she called every couple of months. Never asked about her dancing. Never asked about where she was living and working. Never asked about the aunt. Are you singing? her mother would ask. They were always extremely brief phone calls, as far as I could tell, and Juliana would skip a meal afterward, starve herself more than usual. And then ask me to take her to a movie the next weekend, a rare outing.

What made me think of the singing? It doesn't matter. It is a Saturday morning, the day that I brought her to my college the first time. I've gotten up early, anxious, and pass the waiting at my dormitory window. I remember that window well. I remember the flaking white trim, the leaded glass panes slightly beveled at the edges, the latch that didn't fit. I spent many hours at that window. It framed my heart. I sat there on the window seat alone, gazing out, at what? Trying to imagine my future in the gently rolling soccer field? Trying to make sense of the cataclysms in my body, the weight of fresh love and anxiety? Trying to connect the infinity of time before I was born to the infinity of time after I would be dead? I see the familiar window, the rolling playing fields beyond. And I see the boy, the young man.

It is a Saturday, a day she usually spends on the week's

shopping for her aunt. When he meets her at the bus station, she throws her arms around his neck and says that she is happy despite the awful trip.

"You look tired," he says.

"I am a little," she answers. "But I want to see everything. Show me all of your beautiful places. I'll pretend that I'm a student here. I see the college students at NYU, and I know just how they walk. I can walk just like a college girl." She prances a few steps ahead of him, swinging her hips. "See, I can be a college girl if I want to."

He gives her a bouquet of fresh flowers, which she cradles in one arm and carries like a prom queen.

Burnt autumn leaves lie scattered on the paths of the college grounds. It is a football weekend, and students and their dates promenade about the campus, flirting and laughing and honking their pig horns. The paths smell of beer. From open dormitory windows, a drunken hodgepodge of music.

Holding her dear hand in his, he strolls with her to the grassy courtyard between Davis and Smith, to the chapel at the moment its bell begins chiming, to the stately row of poplars along the diagonal path, everywhere they go drawing the covetous stares of his classmates. Does she enjoy being the center of attention? Cunningham, without feminine accompaniment as usual, Wayne Manning wearing only his offensive T-shirt despite the cool weather, Phillipe Renault with his slick hair and sexy French manner, all want to meet her. They talk to her a little too long, and he will not let go of her free hand.

Professor Galloway passes on the way to his campus office, and he too stops to chat. Like the others, he seems smitten with her. "So this is your hour of eternity," he says to Charles, looking at her. She blushes. How dare Galloway refer to his love poem to her. What will she think, that he has shared his poem with everyone on campus? To heighten the insult, Galloway reaches into his briefcase and gives Juliana one of his own sappy poems.

CHARLES pulls her away. They have only a few hours, and he wants her to himself.

"Come with me," he says. "We'll need flashlights."

He takes her across campus to the physics building, down wooden stairs to the ancient basement, to the end of the corridor and into the dark room. "No electricity in here, at least no working lights. It must have been the original basement for the old college." The room smells of oil, graphite, dust, and age.

"What is this place? It's freezing."

He thinks it was some kind of storage room for scientific equipment. Seventy-five years ago, maybe more. He slowly drags the beam of his flashlight across the strange instruments on the shelves, illuminating one by one the glass jars with electrical wires winding out of them, great brass spheres mounted on poles, coils of wire as fine as a spider's silk, batteries the size of footlockers, wheels geared to other wheels geared to pulleys and cranks, silver canisters and plates, tubes and globulars, metallic cylinders connected by a maze of brass rods, glass bubbles with intricate twists and protrusions, brass microscopes, brass telescopes, prisms, enormous glass disks held in the grip of sharp metal claws. These are sacred objects, cast away by a prior civilization.

"They're beautiful," she says. "Even more beautiful because I don't know what any of them do."

"Yes." He shines his flashlight on a huge silver ball, and he sees her in the spray of the light. He loves her pleasure at what he has shown her, like her pleasure when he reads poetry to her. Or the way that she crawls beside him on the cot in the ballerinas' dressing room.

They walk the perimeter of the room, following the beam of their flashlight. As if in a church, they talk in whispers, their voices absorbed in the dark cavities of this place, which he discovered his freshman year and has told no one about, like the inside of his body. It is his secret, now hers.

Here they are far from maps, people, the world of tables and chairs. He asks if she misses the town where she grew up in Virginia, and she says that she misses the mountains, their blue gauziness, how the mountains melted out of the sky in early morning. She would like to take him there, she says, and he laughs, knowing that it will never happen. She says she would like just one mountain, a small one, outside her window in Manhattan, a height she can sleep against, a quiet against the sounds of buses and cars. That is all that she misses about Virginia. He misses Lake Michigan, he tells her, the way that it looked different every single day, like a new person. He misses eating breakfast with his parents on their little porch in the summer. He misses his sister's hair in the sink. But he and Juliana are here now, together. Here.

He wants to show her something that she will never forget. Giving her his flashlight to hold, he cranks a handle at the base of one of the glass disks. Faster. Sparks begin flying from the metallic claws, like miniature lightning. He cranks harder. The disk glows a dull blue, a giant blue eye in the night, a blue moon. The air crackles. He keeps cranking. Now her face is lit in the blue light, her skin turns blue, like the time they made love on the floor of the studio, with blue neon light coming through the window and painting her body.

REUNION

She closes her eyes, holds on to him. When she first moved in with her aunt, she says, a lightning storm came in the night, and she hid terrified until her aunt took her into the big bed and told her that lightning was the sewing thread of the angels. Blue threads. Now her closed eyelids are blue.

"Kiss me," she whispers. "Do you know that I am happy with you? To be here with you."

NINE

LATER that afternoon, when they walk along the college paths, the sunlight seems unnatural. Hand in hand, they stroll through the President's Garden. The asters are still blooming, and their slender pink petals reaching out from their tawny-colored hearts remind him of her.

"Stay the night with me," he whispers. She doesn't answer. "Don't you want to?"

They sit on a bench by the Baston stone fountain, near enough that they can feel a slight mist on their cheeks. He notices the lovely way that she folds her hands on her lap, the long curve of her neck. Since leaving the basement of lightning, she has seemed distracted. What is the matter? he asks.

"City Ballet won't give me an audition," she says.

"Why not?"

"Balanchine doesn't give reasons. There are hundreds of dancers who want to dance with City Ballet. But I'll get an audition."

"Maybe Balanchine's not taking any new people."

A shadow of irritation crosses her face. "Don't talk down to me. Of course he takes new people. I'll get an audition. Tony says that I'm getting better and better. He's started giving me private lessons on Sundays. Miss Magay saw me dance last week. I'll get into City Ballet. I've got to push harder, that's all."

He finds himself annoyed with her. Most immediately because she will not stay the night. In two months she has never allowed him more than a few hours with her when she was not dancing or working. Not once has she given up a class or rehearsal to spend time with him. And now her Sundays will be occupied as well.

"I'm hungry," she says and takes from her purse her white Tupperware food container, with its hard-boiled egg, carrot, and piece of bread.

For a moment he wants to fling her birdlike crumbs to the ground, carry her back to the physics basement, hold

her prisoner there, force her to his will. Sometimes he hates
it that she is a dancer.

BUT at other moments he wishes instead that he were a
dancer himself so that he could partner her in *Swan Lake*
and *Les Patineurs* and all the other ballets that he's never
heard of. So that he could spend every second with her.
Much of her life remains a mystery to him. He knows nothing of her mother, not even a picture, nothing of the life
that she lived growing up, nothing of her friends besides
Lynn. When he tells her about himself, she doesn't want to
know. Each time they make love in the ballerinas' dressing
room, he sits at her counter after she's gone and picks up
her combs and face creams and lipsticks. What is he searching for? What piece of her is here? He wants her photograph, her hairbrush, her bra.

Each time they get stoned together on the fire-escape
landing, he hopes that she will open up to him. Open in
the lazy vapor of the marijuana and spill. Two o'clock in
the morning. They sit on cardboard boxes, look out on the
brick backs of other brick buildings, other fire-escape lad-
ders that slither down to the ground like dark snakes. Sky
and stars touch the dark rooftops. She is singing, so softly
that he cannot hear the words. Kiss me, she says sleepily.

Here. And here. Please tell me, he says. About what? About you. I don't tell anyone about me. Between silences they sift through the boxes: discarded costumes, worn toe shoes, empty perfume bottles, playing cards, newspapers and magazines, dead batteries, phonograph records, string, wine bottles, lamps. A jumble of secrets, like her.

Early morning. Gently she disentangles their bodies. She leans down over the edge of the cot and puts on her toe shoes, leads him half asleep out of the ballerinas' dressing room and into the dark, silent studio. Without saying a word, she begins dancing. He watches, her audience of one, watches her move in the small light of the neon sign outside the window. Her energy startles him. She flies. She flutters. She spins the thick strands of blackness around her. Where has he found this beautiful dim ghost? Her body glows with a haunting light. At times she disappears into an inky corner of the room, then comes bounding out, twirling and leaping, her feet tiny taps on the floor. She is a sudden poem, the froth of a wave, the lacy flicker of a star. "You are everything," he says. He watches, spellbound, while she dances, while the waking sounds of the city start to stir and the room slowly fills with the dawn. Finally she rushes to him, panting, glistening, and throws herself into his arms. "I am alive," she says between gasps. "I have felt heaven."

———

INSPIRED by her, he has written a new poem:

If I were a piece of clay
I would bend beneath your hands
and leave a moistness
on your sleeve.
Your fingers and palms would gray,
you could never travel from your home
without my scent.
And I. The blind would know
my shapes, my indentations,
the blind would know your hands.
You would come into your room
of glass and light
and say
this is how I touch a chair,
a book, a leaf.
But how poor to be that chair,
that book, that leaf
left without a trace
as if a breath without the push of air
as if a wound without a scar.

REUNION

While I curve beneath your touch,
changed forever,
moving statue of your hands.
Sing my bending.

ON a cold weekend in December she finally takes him to meet her aunt. The apartment is even smaller than he imagined it, with a sitting room barely large enough for its faded sofa and two chairs, a tiny efficiency kitchen with a two-burner stove. An aroma of cooked tomatoes and garlic hovers in the still air. The aunt stares at him sharply as he tries to squeeze his overcoat into the closet, which is packed with books and old leotards and toe shoes. Then, giving up on the closet, he sits with Juliana on the sofa.

The aunt takes his small gift and puts it unopened on a table. "Juliana tells me you're studying poetry," she says. Her voice is slow and refined.

He nods.

"Poetry is as useless as ballet," the aunt says and smiles. Her mouth is delicate, like the rest of her face, and he can tell that she was once a beautiful woman.

"Why say something like that, Kik?" says Juliana.

"Because it's true," says the aunt. She begins coughing. After a few moments she catches her breath. "I didn't say it was unimportant. I just said it was useless. What do you say, Charles? Why are you studying such a useless subject? Or don't you agree with me?" She stares at him again with her intense eyes, eyes like Juliana's without the heavy black eyeliner.

She's testing him. "Poetry is a form of perfection," he says, "something beautiful. I don't know what use it has. Why do things need a use? Poetry helps me understand the world." He could say more, but he fears that he will sound grandiose. Taking off his scarf, he reaches for Juliana. Immediately the aunt fixes her gaze on their clasped hands.

"So you've made it this far," says the aunt. "Juliana doesn't bring many of her male friends to meet me. But I wish she would."

"Don't say that when you don't mean it," says Juliana.

"Certainly I've met some of the dancers," says the aunt. "Oh yes. Handsome young men." She smooths her fine silver hair. "But the problem, of course, is that Juliana has no time for socializing. She's a dancer. She's my little dancer, my little courageous dancer, not so little anymore. Have you seen her dance? But what am I saying, you've surely seen her dance. Isn't she wonderful! She entered Magay when she was sixteen. Do you know how many girls would like to dance with Magay?"

"I'm going to City," says Juliana.

"Yes, dearest," the aunt says, looking at him. "You'll do anything that you want to do. You always have."

He notices a photograph on the sofa table, a scene at the beach. In the background, swimmers lounge on the sand, a strip of ocean, a strip of sky. In the foreground, the aunt. She poses with a little girl, another woman, and a man. All of them wear swimsuits, the women with white hats, the man with goggles around his neck. All of them seem to have taken in too much sun, and their faces are flushed and depleted. Around the neck of the aunt floats a fragile necklace of small stones, white dots against her pink skin. Her hair, lustrous and brown, touches her bare shoulders. The other woman has wild eyes too large for her face and an odd tilt of her head and looks like she would rather be somewhere else. The man, forlorn, has an uncertain relation to the two women. Could he be a boyfriend, or a brother? Smack in the center, her mouth open in a howl, is the little girl, unmistakably Juliana. Somehow she seems the oldest of the group. She alone is aware that she's been photographed. She's been pinned by the camera, and she screams for her freedom. She's the red speck that burns a hole in the picture.

"I see you looking at the photo," says the aunt. "Atlantic City. A prick in time, ages ago. Sometimes I think that moment in the photo never happened, that part of my life. I'm not sure that it did. Have you traveled, Charles? I went to Greece once, also on the ocean. There's a tiny island there called Kea, with an ancient lion carved right out of the rock. It's quite surprising. You should see it someday."

The aunt begins coughing again. She stands up. Evidently the visit is over. "I put the grocery list in your bag," she says to Juliana. "No hurry." She takes Juliana aside. "Remember, dearest, to get the Swinson cheddar, not the Kraft. It comes in a green container. And I want the thirty-five-yard roll of the Reynolds Wrap. Don't get the sixty-six-yard roll. Okay? Enjoy the afternoon with your young man." She turns to Charles and smiles and holds out her hand to him.

"Thank you," he says.

"There's nothing to thank me for," she says. She pauses. "You know, it doesn't matter what happens to me. But Juliana is going to keep dancing. Dancing is her life. I hope you understand that."

"Come, Charles, let's go," Juliana says.

OUTSIDE it has begun to snow, a snow so light that it melts soon after touching the street, yet the cars have turned on their windshield wipers and headlights. Plainly the aunt has tried to discourage him. But he won't be discouraged. Juliana loves him, she has told him so. Does the aunt understand that? Juliana has told him she loves him. He puts his arm around her waist as they walk down the sidewalk. For a few moments they pause in front of a man selling brass Christmas bells under a snow-dusted awning. The man has spread out his bells on a table and is jingling them one by one.

This afternoon they will shop, then have an evening together. A movie, perhaps dancing at a disco, or an art opening somewhere, he doesn't care. Through her he is learning who he is. He is her "sensitive college boy," she tells him. She says that he is arrogant at times but willing to admit his mistakes, that he is serious but can laugh, that he allows himself to be hurt, which he shouldn't do, that he wants to do something important in the world but doesn't know what it could be. He is in love. Before now he has understood nothing about the world. Now it begins. He draws her closer to him, close enough to smell her hair in the cold air, the lavender of her skin.

What is she saying at this moment? He listens, watches the movement of her lips. In the last three months he has memorized every word that she's said to him and written it down in his writer's journal, sprinkled between the scratchy drafts of his poems.

Why do you ask me so many questions?

I'll never be a great dancer. Never.

On a rain-splattered page: *You love me too much. It's not good for you to love me so much.*

Would you kill yourself if you had to stop writing poems? I would kill myself if I had to stop dancing.

I want you to write a poem with your you-know-what. Here, on my stomach. Here.

By December 7 she has told him she loves him twenty-three times and told him she doesn't love him seventeen times.

He hasn't written down the words he's said to her because he doesn't remember them precisely, and he wants to be precise about words, as precise as the curve of her eyebrow, or the tiny, caramel-colored mole on her upper lip. Or sometimes he does write down his words to her, as he wanted to say them, or as he might have said them, beautiful and melodious words, and he has memorized these too, and wondered how we ever know for sure what was said or not said, what was thought or not thought. Because every possible word is said and not said, every possible thought is thought and not thought, and what is not said is still there, like the shape of space around the edge of a leaf. Sometimes he wonders if the not-love of space around his love for her is stronger than the love.

On the front of his journal, he has spelled out her name with letters cut from the title pages of his textbooks. "J" from *Existentialism: Dostoevsky to Jaspers*. "u" from *Modern European History*. "l" from *Introduction to Biology*.

The snow is a lace handkerchief on her hair. Unexpectedly she tells him that she has in her purse two tickets to a performance of the New York City Ballet that evening, Suzanne Farrell in *The Nutcracker*. "She's only three years older than me," says Juliana as they walk back from the market with their shopping bags. "She started dancing with Balanchine at sixteen, the same age I started with Magay." She laughs bitterly. "Balanchine makes ballets just for her. He's obsessed with her. He doesn't let her out of his sight. You know, all of his principal ballerinas sleep with him. She's forty years younger than he is." He leans over and kisses her in a long embrace that makes people stare.

That evening, as soon as they take their seats in the glittering performance hall, he feels her stiffening. He tries to hold her hand, but she withdraws. She doesn't even take off her coat. "What's wrong?" he asks. She will not answer. Then, when the ballet starts, she is transfixed. She becomes a frozen statue, scarcely breathing, pointed at the stage. The *Nutcracker* story is less interesting to him than the narrative of *Swan Lake,* but he is mesmerized by the bodies themselves and the emotional changes from one scene to the next. And the bodies are fantastic, chiseled sculptures in motion.

From the reaction of the audience, he knows the instant that Suzanne Farrell glides onto the stage as the Sugar Plum Fairy, beautiful, tall and pale like white marble, with heavily darkened eyes and wearing a short tinsel tutu that glitters with jewels. Farrell is a kaleidoscope of form. Moment to moment she changes from limpid and serene to cloudy and voluptuous, first fine porcelain and then a white steed. Her impossibly long legs swing like a weighted pendulum, daringly off balance yet completely controlled. She is the brightest star in the constellation of stars, a goddess to the other goddesses.

After her first pas de deux, people clap and cheer. One aficionado is so overwhelmed that he cannot hold back his bouquet for the end of the ballet but flings it immediately at the stage, leaving a trail of roses atop people's heads.

Charles looks over at Juliana and sees that she is crying.

"WHAT'S this room?"

I'm startled. A woman and three men, including Michael Bisi, have just stumbled into the Trustees Room, all wearing their pig snouts and tails. From twenty feet away I can smell the alcohol.

"Sorry," says one of the men when he sees me. He mumbles something to the woman, and she giggles. "We were just wandering around."

"Charles!" says Michael Bisi. His pin-striped shirt is hanging loose out of his pants. "What are you doing here? You coming to the dinner at the boathouse?"

"I don't know," I say.

"I'll save you a seat," says Michael. "You just missed a goddamned boring lecture by some goddamned boring linguist."

"I like this room," says the woman. "It's cozy. It's the coziest room I've ever seen. You look all by your lonesome, Charles."

"Don't be so nosy," says the man next to her. "Come on, let's go."

The woman walks over to the recessed alcove and taps her fingernails against the glass cabinet. "Look at those old books."

"Lanie. Let's go."

"Okay," says Lanie. "Don't rush me. Bye, lonesome Charles."

They glance around the room, turn, and leave. "Save you a seat," Michael calls out. For a few moments I hear their feet shuffling in the hallway, whispers and laughing, and then they are gone.

TEN

Too soon the Christmas vacation arrives, longer than it has ever been, two weeks of separation from her at his family house in Michigan. His air has been cut off. In a state of urgency, he calls her every day at five-fifteen, after rehearsal and before she starts work at Frankie's. On the telephone she seems distant, occupied, unable to say the intimacies that he wants to hear. This is part of his anguish, he thinks, and perhaps hers as well.

Each night he dreams of her, dreams of her body next to his, and then awakes before dawn to find that his bed is empty.

To fill up the days, he writes poems and works on his

senior paper on the spirituality of Emily Dickinson, all of his books spread out on the stained carpet of his bedroom. Spirituality not in the theological sense but in the more abstract sense of the inner self and a consciousness of something larger than we are. So much more he now understands. *The Spirit is the Conscious Ear . . . For other Services—as Sound—There hangs a smaller Ear Outside the Castle.* The conscious ear. Yes, he can hear what he has not heard before, a soft throbbing, the pulse of the world. E.D. must have been in love to understand these things. How else could she have known about spirituality. Even in her isolation, the world flowed through her veins, she felt every joy and sorrow and breath of humanity. And she must have suffered, as he is beginning to suffer.

In a flash of discovery, he decides to compare her work to that of William Blake, her forerunner in verse of the spirit. *Little Fly Thy summer's play My thoughtless hand Has brush'd away. Am not I A fly like thee? Or art not thou A man like me?* He thinks E.D. must have read Blake. The two minds move parallel to each other. Both visionary and spiritual and rebellious in their way. In both, childlike simplicity gives way to hidden meanings. He will impress Professor Galloway with his comparison.

"Lester is home," his mother says to him at lunch. "Why don't you go see him?" She sits with him at the kitchen table, wearing the cross-country ski jacket that his father has given her for Christmas even though it's boiling in the house. She stares at him while he eats. He feels that she disapproves of everything he does.

"I will. We're going to a party at Piedmont on Tuesday night." There. Lester was always her favorite. Glad that he's pleased her, he tells her about his idea to compare Emily Dickinson and William Blake. Yes, of course she knows Emily Dickinson. She nods and smiles, wanting to understand, but she cannot hide her puzzlement. Is that what he does behind his closed door each day? She seems almost embarrassed to hear about his poetical studies. Suddenly she looks old in the thin winter light. The familiar scar above her left eye has merged with a long crease across her forehead. She's forty-six.

Juliana's reserve on the telephone has made him irritable. And he feels cramped in this small little house, with its five little rooms and its milky linoleum floors and the television constantly going. His mother is cramped. No wonder she goes out into the woods to ski every morning. For years they've been talking about moving into a bigger house. Prices are low in Ludington. They could certainly afford a larger house, but they stay here, year after year. Somehow his mother remains optimistic about her life. Ever since moving away from her own parents and her brothers, she has carefully nurtured a blind loyalty to his father. She likes the same movies that he likes, she likes the same food, she likes and dislikes the same people. She would move into an even smaller house if he wanted.

"Charles. Who is that you call every afternoon?"

"Juliana. I've told you about Juliana before."

"I didn't know you two were so close."

"Yes."

His mother pauses. From her hesitation, from the way that she twists her mouth, he knows that she does not approve.

"What are her friends like?" she asks.

"She hangs out with dancers. That's what they're into. All her friends are dancers."

Now his mother's mouth is really twisting, but she's holding it back. He looks at her, wondering how she's holding it back, and notices that she's actually sweating from the heat, but she won't take off the jacket. "Take off your jacket, Mom," he says.

"You don't seem happy after you call her," she says.

"I am happy." He wants to talk to his mother about Juliana. He wants to be able to talk to his mother about how he feels, about the poems that he's writing. He wants to shake her.

She reaches across the table and holds his hand.

The day before New Year's, Charles receives in the mail his grades for the first semester: A in American Poets, A in Existentialism, C in Modern European History, D in Biology. As expected, he is good at the useless and poor at the rest. His parents will not be pleased. For a moment he contemplates sending Juliana's aunt the report, a comic confirmation of her assessment of him, but then he rips up the letter with its engraved college insignia and tosses the shreds in his old catcher's mitt.

WHEN he returns to college in January, he is desperate to see her. But she cannot receive him on Wednesday, their usual day. Thursday? No, not Thursday, she says gently, without explanation. Friday? Possibly Friday, she says. She will call him back. No, tell me now, he shouts into the telephone. Let me come on Friday. Don't you want to see me? You sound so angry, she says. Of course I want to see you. Then why don't you make time for me? he asks miserably. I love you, she says. I make as much time as I can. Come on Friday.

When he meets her late Friday night at Frankie's, she looks exhausted, her face moist and pink from the oven heat of the restaurant, her delicate shoulders sagging from the burden of carrying trays for six hours. He wants to wrap his arms around her, to overwhelm her with his love and desire, but the moment doesn't seem right, and he contents himself with holding the hand that she offers. She barely speaks to him. Why will she not embrace him? Hasn't she longed for him during the several weeks of separation as he's longed for her? In silence they walk along the street, illuminated by Christmas lights still blinking in shop-windows. An occasional taxi cruises by with its glowing medallion and weary passenger inside.

In the subway another wave of desire and anguish moves through him. The more distant she seems, the more he wants her. He imagines their future together. Of course, he will need to move to New York, as much as he dislikes the crush of the city. As soon as possible, he must get a job and save her from these terrible nights. And he must hire the best ballet teacher in the country.

"Juliana." He will tell her about his plans. But she is staring out of the black window, too tired to talk. Even now she is beautiful.

In the ballerinas' dressing room, she takes off her clothes and begins washing herself in the sink, rubbing a soapy sponge along the length of her body while he watches. She shines in the light.

"What is this?" he asks, touching a small bruise on her hip.

"I bumped into the piano a few days ago," she says. "It's nothing."

He stoops and kisses the bruise. "You are too sweet to me," she says. She draws him to her, her wet breasts against his shirt, then resumes bathing.

"The ballerinas should have a shower," he says, watching her.

"There are a lot of things we should have. Miss Magay barely has enough money to rent the studio. We have no insurance. We get paid only two weeks a year, during performance, not near enough to live on. This is a second-rate company. Or haven't you figured that out by now."

"After I have a job," he says, "you won't have to work anymore. And you can get lessons from somebody better than Tony. I've been asking around."

"Don't, Charles. Please don't plan my life."

She dries herself with a towel and stands nude in front of the mirror. She has wounded him. Sometimes she speaks to him as if he were almost a stranger. He wants to ravish her, he wants to pour his heart out to her, but she seems a thousand miles away.

"Juliana."

"What is it?"

He hesitates. Can he try again to talk to her, truly talk to her? "I found that Greek island your aunt was speaking about," he says abruptly. "With the prehistoric lion. Kea."

"Yes, what about it?"

"I asked a friend who has family in Greece. I thought maybe your aunt made it up."

"I always liked that name," she says. "It's a pretty name." Then she turns from the mirror and looks into his eyes. She does love him, he can see. Why has he ever doubted that?

Now she seems eager for him. She unbuttons his shirt, pulls his trousers down to the floor, lets him lay her out on the folding cot in the corner. Shivers run up and down her body while he covers her with kisses. She pulls him on top of her and guides him into her.

Not the explosion of their first lovemaking, not quite like that, but passionate and sweet, a slow wheeling flight. Afterward she rests in his arms and traces his eyebrow with her finger.

"Recite some poetry to me," she murmurs.

A wind has blown the leaves
Across the autumn way
And I, a child now lost,
Must wait for Mother's say.

"It's so simple, but lovely," she says. "Is it one of yours?"

"Yes. It's the first stanza of a longer poem. This one rhymes."

"You're going to be a great writer someday."

"I'm not so sure about that."

"Yes you will. I'm sure about it. And when you are, I want you to remember that I helped inspire you. Will you remember that? Will you remember that you recited your beautiful poetry to me, here?"

He takes her hand and kisses her fingertips one by one. For hours they lie together in that way. As if the several weeks' separation had never existed. He cannot remember the trip home at Christmas, the lonely weeks with his parents, even where he was this morning. Is it so basic as this? Is lovemaking the beginning and the end? The conquerer of fear and anger and jealousy and deprivation, the essence of human experience?

At six she dresses and leaves. He remains sprawled on the cot, happy, his eyes slowly sweeping the tiny room that has become their private sanctuary and blessing. The counter covered with bottles and creams, the postcards and scribbled notes taped to the mirror, the good-luck charms dangling from the stage lights, the brass costume rack in the corner, the warped wooden floorboards littered with shoes and old program announcements and bits of cloth. Here he is at home. He picks up a scrap of paper from the floor. "Wave Felice off," it says in a flowery script. Another scrap has a telephone number. Oddly, the number begins with the same area code and extension as his college. The handwriting looks like Juliana's. But who could she be calling at the college but him? Idly, he dresses.

I watch him dress, and I want to speak to him. Can I? He is like my child. I want to talk to him now, at this instant, before . . . "Don't. Don't," I would say. I want to warn him. "The channel branch is ahead." But what a silly idea to think I can warn him. His future is already past. We cannot change what has happened, can we. We cannot talk to ourselves at a prior moment in time. Still, I want to warn him. He is so fragile, like her. But his heart is more open. Although he thinks he is happy, he is suffering. He has suffered, he is suffering, he will suffer. I am dizzy with present and past. And future. What year is it?

Shadows stretch across the floor and up the wall like frozen men. I'm not sure where I am. The Trustees Room, yes. But it must be early evening now. The place has grown dim, the light from the window has faded. And I no longer hear voices in the next room. Weren't they playing billiards a few minutes ago? Cunningham and the others must have left for the big dinner at the boathouse. I should leave too.

Where is my jacket? Did I bring a jacket? I look around the room. In the syrupy dusk light, I see two chairs, a conference table, the shape of a sofa, a lamp, faint bookshelves on the opposite wall, a security light glowing softly in the corner. And there the model of the college, almost completely in shadow. I should leave. I want to leave. I am terrified by what I have seen. The endless potentialities held dangling by threads. I have been a forced voyeur, paralyzed, watching the destruction, the destruction that has happened and the destruction that will happen. I have been forced to watch as I strangle myself and am strangled by others. But who has forced me to watch? The beautiful twenty-two-year-old boy, full of magic and life and the power of not knowing the future. That's it, isn't it, the true source of his power: that his future remains unknown to him.

I squint into the shadows, the tiny walkways and buildings. I cannot look away. I feel the destruction, I want to rub it all over my body.

THROUGHOUT the weekend, he thinks on and off about the telephone number. He wants to forget it. At one point on Sunday, as he walks to the gymnasium for his afternoon workout, he almost tosses the scrap of paper into a trash bin. Perhaps it isn't Juliana's handwriting at all.

Later that evening, after returning from the library, he begins searching through the campus directory. Six or seven thousand telephone numbers and names. After forty minutes he has discovered a match. James Galloway. He rechecks the number. With an appalling clarity, he recalls the way Galloway looked at Juliana when he briefly met her on the campus. Galloway could have slipped her his telephone number. But she might never have called him. Certainly Juliana must be accustomed to unwanted advances. Or perhaps the note isn't Juliana's at all. A string of accidents. But a hazy dread settles in his stomach, and he turns over and over in his bed for the rest of the night.

In the morning, sleepless and brooding, he skips his first class. He feels both foolish and hurt at the same time. Should he ask Juliana about Galloway's telephone number?

Instead he decides to observe Galloway himself. At the next class of American Poets II, he examines every aspect of his professor. Asks himself: Could Galloway be carrying on an adulterous affair with the girlfriend of one of his students, a girl half his age? It seems impossible.

He carefully studies Galloway's manner as he saunters up and down the aisles, wearing his seductive black turtleneck. Does Galloway appear happier, sadder, guilty? How does adultery show in a man's face? Does his gait appear more adventurous than usual? His eyes, always heavy-lidded, do indeed seem a bit more worn than a few months ago. Could he be fatigued from his late-night trysts with Juliana? The thought makes Charles feel dirty.

"'I make a virtue of my suffering,'" Galloway recites from Robert Frost, his most cherished poet.

From nearly everything that goes on round me.
In other words, I know wherever I am,
Being the creature of literature I am,
I shall not lack for pain to keep me awake.

"Frost accepts both pleasure and pain as part of life," says Galloway, leaning back handsomely against his desk. "But he seems to be happier with pain. No, *happy* is not quite the right word. Frost recognizes that literature, and life, are elevated by pain. Thus he makes a virtue of suffering."

Could Galloway be talking about himself? Charles wonders. Galloway is a "creature of literature," is he not? A vague suffering hangs over him, has always hung over him. He has an unsatisfying marriage, a wife who will not mingle with his students or listen to him recite his maudlin poetry. The pain keeps him awake. And then what? What does Professor Galloway do with the pain that keeps him awake? Does he attempt to smother it under his pillow? Does he confess his dissatisfactions to his wife? Or does he go prowling in the night like some dark weasely animal, offering his telephone number to beautiful young women half his age?

Galloway is still talking. "I would imagine that none of you young men quite understands this virtue of suffering, this elevation by pain. It's not your fault. You haven't lived long enough." He pauses. "Perhaps you've been in love. Or think you've been in love." Galloway gestures toward the window to illustrate his point. Does he wave his arms more grandly than usual? Nothing is certain. And why did he mention love? To Charles, his face, his words, his gestures all seem suspicious.

After class Charles follows his professor, remaining out of sight. Galloway goes to his office across campus and shuts the door. Trailing behind, Charles stations himself outside the closed door like an admiring student, and pretends to read a book. What is Galloway doing inside? A shadow slides across the frosted glass panel of the closed door. A light goes on. After a few minutes he hears Galloway's voice. The professor has made a telephone call. Charles inches closer to the door to hear what his professor is saying: "camera" and "Friday." A desk drawer opens and closes. Then another telephone call. He hears "Smallenback," or something like that, "session," "bulletin." What is he looking for? Surely Galloway wouldn't be talking to Juliana at one o'clock in the afternoon. At one o'clock in the afternoon Juliana is dancing.

He stands outside the office another hour, waiting for something. Then Galloway's steps approach the door, Charles flies down the hall and around a corner.

The next day he again stalks Galloway on campus, follows him secretively to and from his office, huddles outside the closed office door. Although he discovers nothing for certain, his suspicions enlarge Galloway's little routines into a flagrant rush of guilty actions: an entrance into the building by a side door, a bag delivered to his office, a surprising digression during his lecture, an overly long trip to the toilet. On his way across campus one day, Galloway unexpectedly stops to make a call at a pay telephone in the student center. Around the corner, Charles hears him laugh, and then: "You little witch you . . ."

WHEN he visits Juliana the next week, Charles feels edgy and uncomfortable. Perhaps he can coax something from her without a direct confrontation.

"Do you remember that professor we met at the college a few months ago?" he asks as they lie entwined on the folding cot. "James Galloway."

REUNION

"Yes, I remember him," says Juliana.

Her tone is neutral, subdued, disinterested. Yet why did she answer so quickly? If Galloway means nothing to her, why did she remember him without any pause, without the usual gentle shake of the memory when one tries to recall some insignificant event months ago? He will press a little further.

"You do remember him."

"Yes," she says. "What of it?" She pulls a sheet over her bare legs, their legs.

"I was just wondering." He hesitates. "He seemed quite taken with you." Unconsciously his body braces itself for the worst. He waits, unable to see her face. He waits for her to say something more, but she doesn't, and he has already said too much himself.

LATER that week, after the torment of uncertainty has grown still more ugly, he decides that he will watch Galloway's comings and goings at night. Borrowing Nick Blanchard's car, he parks across the street from Galloway's house at nine o'clock in the evening, turns out the lights, but keeps the engine running for heat. As the dark hours pass uneventfully, he listens to the radio, he leans back on a pillow he has brought from his room, he smokes cigarettes, and he curses himself for being such a fool. One way or the other, he is a fool.

At daybreak, cold and tired, he drives back to campus, takes a shower, and goes to his morning classes. In the student center he pleads with Ralph Cunningham to help him in the vigil that night. "You're out of your gourd," says Ralph. "And besides, it's illegal what you're doing. A word from the wise. Cease and desist."

That night, as Charles sits on the lookout in Nick's car, Galloway comes out of his house at ten o'clock and drives away. Charles's first impulse is to follow, but he decides that he may be seen. So he waits in the dark. Quite possibly Galloway is going out to get some small item at the all-night store around the corner. Charles will wait. He begins tearing one of the road maps into pieces. When it has become bits of confetti, he starts on another map. Then another. His own mind is slowly shredding.

At eight o'clock the next morning, Galloway returns.

An unlikely coincidence of events? Does Galloway have an all-night poker game somewhere? Or an ill mother who needs company while she sleeps? The impossible now seems possible. Without wanting to, he imagines Galloway's drive out of town, the long silent trip on the highway and the occasional road signs glowing in the dark, finally coming into New York through the tunnel and south to Greenwich Village. He imagines Galloway walking up the stone steps above the bodega, meeting Juliana at the entrance to the dance studio, being led by her to the rear, to the ballerinas' dressing room. The door opens, they kiss. Does she undress him? Does she bite his shoulder and rub her nipples against his chest? How can it be? He can imagine it, and at the same time he can't imagine it.

SLEEPLESS, unshaven, he takes the next bus to New York. So many times he has ridden this bus, he knows the worn metal steps, the ads on the wall for cosmetics and night school, the filthy cramped seats. He waits for her on the street below the Magay dance studio, sits on a rough concrete step and sweeps aside the cigarette butts and greasy food wrappers. Dirt and cold mean nothing. His insides are on fire. Every second something new is destroyed.

After an eternity, dancers begin entering the building for the start of rehearsal. They walk past his stoop and stare at him quizzically. A blur of scarves and mittens, heavy coats, boots. He nods dumbly. The smell of roast pork and sausage, urine. Strange that the senses continue to work when thoughts have been suffocated. He pictures her face the first time he saw her, angelic. Lying. He hates her, as he hates Galloway. But he loves her as well.

Then he sees her coming down the street.

"What are you doing here?" she asks, startled. Then she softens and smiles. "What a surprise." Her breath makes little gray clouds in the cold air.

It could still be untrue. Let it be untrue. A terrible nightmare. He slowly stands, his legs numb from sitting an hour in the cold. Can he see into her? He realizes that he's never been able to see into her.

"Come up with me to rehearsal," she says.

"We have to talk."

"You know that I have rehearsal now. I had no idea you were coming today. Walk up with me. We can talk at the break." She reaches for his hand with a turquoise knitted glove.

Still untrue. If he forgets, if he forgets everything, can he imagine himself back to the world before?

"Listen to me," he says. Something about his voice stops her. She stops in the frozen air and stands still and waits for what he has to say.

"Do you love me?" he asks. An odd place to begin. He has surprised himself.

"Of course I love you." They take a few steps past the entrance to the building and stand in front of a small pastry shop, closed and barricaded with an iron grating. "I got a new leotard since the last time you saw me," she says. "My other one was way too green. It made me feel like a bug."

He studies her face: the little beauty mark on her lip that he knows so well, the heavily darkened eyelashes, the green eyes.

"Do you love anybody else? Any other men?"

"Why should that matter? I love you."

"Tell me. Is there anybody else?"

She hesitates, upset. "I've never asked you that, have I? I never told you that you couldn't have other girlfriends. You have your life and I have my life." She glances back at the entrance to the building. Other dancers are still walking in. "Please, can we talk about this at the break? Rehearsal is beginning."

"Are you seeing James Galloway?" he says, staring at her.

She seems shocked by his question. Yes, he can see shock and guilt on her face. Isn't that guilt? It must be guilt. But she doesn't say anything. She doesn't answer his question.

"Are you sleeping with James Galloway?"

"I don't want to talk about this," she says.

"How can you?" he screams.

"Please."

"Admit it." He rubs his face roughly with his hand. He wants to cut something. "Admit it." She says nothing. "How can you? He's twice your age. He's my professor. How can you fuck Galloway? How can you do this to me?"

"Charles." She takes his hand.

He staggers against the iron grating. "How long has this been going on?"

She doesn't answer, she just holds his hand. Now there are tears in her eyes.

"Do you want to stop seeing me?" she says.

"No," he says miserably. "I love you. I wish I didn't." His head is pounding. What should he say? He doesn't know what to say or how to act. Just hours ago she was in Galloway's arms. Galloway's odor is still smeared on her thighs. "Do you want to break up with me now that you have Galloway?"

"No, I don't want to break up with you."

"So, you have two guys," he shouts. "Maybe more than two. Are there more? Are there more than two? I don't want to know." He looks down and sees her hand in his. How could that be? In the most brutal way, she has betrayed him. He hates her for it, and at the same time he is rotten with knowing that he still worships her, that he cannot leave her.

ELEVEN

THE image of Juliana standing in front of the barricaded shop with tears in her eyes sticks in his heart as he stands in Galloway's office, surrounded by books and framed commendations. Already, without knowing why, he has partly forgiven her. But he can never forgive Galloway, who pretends to be cool even at this moment, even after he has received Charles's ominous phone call. Surely he knows what this meeting is about.

"What can I do for you, Charles?" Galloway says and crosses his arms. But the perennial cloud of sadness hovers over his head, the permanent antihalo. Whatever pleasure he's gotten from fucking Juliana, his life remains unhappy.

"Admit it," Charles shouts. "You are sleeping with her, with Juliana."

"Yes," says Galloway.

The reply has come so swiftly that Charles is momentarily disoriented. Where are words? "How could you?" he says. "You know that she's my girlfriend."

"Of course I know. You introduced us. She was on your arm." Galloway smiles faintly, more a nervous twitch, and lowers himself into the chair behind his desk. He motions to another chair for Charles to sit in.

Charles remains standing. "I don't understand. How could you do such a sleazy thing?"

Galloway sighs. He takes a brass paperweight from his desk, turns it over and over in his hand. "I don't know how to say this. A young woman keeps someone of my age alive. You'll understand in twenty-five years. Beautiful young women . . . they are the flowers of the earth, they make blood flow. They make life. It's not right that they give themselves only to young men. We all need them."

What is this lofty crap? The professor is writing another of his sappy poems to make himself feel good. "Juliana is my girlfriend," Charles shouts. "She's mine. You're screwing my girlfriend. Find somebody else."

"These things aren't so simple," Galloway says softly.

He pauses, gazing at the bookcase in front of him. "You're what, twenty-one years old? Twenty-two years old?" He pauses again, as if searching for words that Charles will understand. "We've made a connection."

"Connection! What connection? I don't believe it. You don't know anything about Juliana. She doesn't love you. She loves me. You're a middle-aged man, and married. You're married. You're cheating on your wife."

"That has nothing to do with it. Please don't give me that antique moral shit."

Charles slams his arm against a bookshelf, causing a dozen books to tumble to the floor. "I want you to stop seeing her. Do you hear me? Stop seeing her."

Galloway smiles again. It is not an arrogant smile, but a melancholy, painful smile. "I can't do that," he says. "I'm sorry. I'm sorry for you. But these things happen. Juliana and I . . . we have something. I need her."

Charles takes a step toward Galloway and grips his upper arm, holds it for a few seconds, then lets go. "If you don't stop seeing her, I'm telling your wife."

"You wouldn't do that," says Galloway. "There's no need to drag my wife into this."

"I'm telling your wife. And I'm going to tell everybody. I'm going to tell President Gray. I'm going to have you thrown out of this place. I'm going to write a letter to the MLA. I hope your career will be ruined. I hope your life will be ruined."

"Please, Charles." Galloway looks at him directly for the first time. "You're going overboard. I know you're upset. We're two men talking here. Let's talk about this like two men."

"Fuck you. I am talking. I'm going to wreck your life. I don't care what happens to you. I'm going to wreck your life."

Galloway stands up from his desk and sweeps back his long hair. Slowly he walks to the window and looks out. "Okay," he says almost in a whisper, his back to Charles. "I'll stop seeing her."

"Now. I want you to stop now."

"Okay. I'll call her tonight and tell her." Galloway turns. His face has lost all of its color. "Can you go now?"

"How do I know you'll stop seeing her?"

"Ask Juliana."

Charles hesitates. "What if she doesn't tell me?" He hates saying this last thing, admitting to Galloway that Juliana is not fully truthful with him.

"Charles, show me some respect. I respect you. You respect me. I'm giving you my word. If you aren't convinced in two weeks that I've stopped seeing her, then expose me. Do whatever you want. I've given you my word."

"Then we have an agreement."

Galloway nods. "Now," he says, "get out of my office."

BUT this isn't at all what I remember. My head is spinning, I am confused. Could I have acted with such savagery? I was naïve, yes, foolish, yes. But I was not a vicious person. Certainly Galloway deserved to be treated viciously. Galloway deserved to be threatened. What I remember is this:

It was a Saturday morning. Or maybe a Sunday, I'm not sure. I called Galloway at his home, early, and said that I had an important matter to discuss with him. In the background I could hear some kind of jazz, a saxophone player. Galloway liked John Coltrane especially. Even on the telephone, without my saying anything about Juliana, I could hear guilt in his voice. He had guessed the purpose of my call.

We met at his office on campus. By this time I was two days without sleep. I hadn't bathed or changed clothes since Thursday. Despite all this, my mind was extremely alert, in the way that anger and jealousy electrify every cell of the body. I was a raw nerve.

Galloway, I could hardly recognize coming down the sleepy hallway. As I remember, he had on a heavy leather jacket and a cowboy hat. It was snowing outside, and a light fringe of snow lay like a fur collar on the shoulders of his coat.

"I've been expecting this," he said as he opened his office door. Yes, the cloud of sadness was there, hanging over his head. I'd never seen him looking so sad before. And the guilt in his eyes. He looked at me briefly and then looked away. Walked to a bookshelf, as if he didn't know what to do with himself, opened a volume of Robert Frost, smiled ironically, then gently returned the book to its place. "Life is expected and unexpected at the same time, isn't it, Charles." I'm pretty sure he said that. After which he slumped behind his desk, made a limp gesture to another chair. I sat down. I almost didn't need to say anything. Everything was there, in the silence between us. He felt my hatred.

"Admit it," I said after a few moments. "You're sleeping with Juliana, aren't you."

"Yes." He fiddled with something on his desk, an ashtray or a pen, or possibly the paperweight. Then he took off his cowboy hat and placed it carefully on the desk.

"How could you do such a sleazy thing?" I said.

Galloway let out a long sigh. "You can say that. Aren't

we all sleazebags? We can't control our impulses. Especially men with beautiful young women. We're animals. All the proper rules of behavior, the ideals, the values, the respect, the self-respect—all of it dissolves into nothing with beautiful young women. You must know this. If you don't know it, you'll know it in twenty-five years."

To my shame, I believe that I felt some kind of bond with him. That's what I remember. He was talking to me about life. Even after what he had done to me, I felt a sympathy. "She's my girlfriend," I said. "You've been screwing my girlfriend."

"Yes," said Galloway. "I don't know what to say. We're animals. I'm sorry for what I've done. I'm sorry for all of us. I'm going to break it off. I'm actually glad that you called me today."

As I remember, someone knocked on the door. I believe it was a cleaning woman who wanted to get in and empty the wastebaskets. Galloway was so upset that he didn't know what to say to her. Rolling her trash can, she pushed into the room, eyed us suspiciously, as if we shouldn't have been there early on a Saturday morning or a Sunday morning, whatever it was, and she emptied the wastebaskets and left.

"How do I know you'll break it off?" I said.

Galloway rose from his desk and went to the window,

stood there looking onto the college grounds. Outside the sun was low and cool, and it skimmed flat along the snowy courtyard and walkways. I could see the stone wall around McMillan, smoke curling away from the chimney of the dining hall. That view is still there, vividly in my memory, and Galloway, standing dark and huge against the window.

"I think my wife knows about this," he said softly, his back to me. "I'm not positive, but I think she does. I'm talking to you in confidence now. Okay? We're two men talking to each other. I didn't want to get involved with Juliana. These things happen. We made a connection. But it's killing me. I have to lie to my wife. This is my second affair. You don't know what it's like lying to your wife again and again. It eats you up. It eats up the trust in a marriage. Clara doesn't trust me anymore."

"Why don't you just tell your wife?" I said. I had my own opinions about Galloway and his wife, a parched marriage. "I'm sorry about your wife. But that has nothing to do with me. What I'm talking about is me and Juliana. I understand what you said about beautiful women. But find somebody else. Find another beautiful young woman. Juliana is mine. I want you to stop seeing her. Now."

Galloway turned from the window to face me. He looked ancient.

"I've already decided to break it off with her. I told her last night. It's not because of you, Charles. I'm not going to pretend to be moral about this. The fact is, you're young, and you've got your entire life in front of you. Whatever happens, you'll get over this. If I really wanted Juliana, I would keep her, no matter what you say. I do need her. But I need the rest of my life more. I'm killing myself. And my wife. I've decided to stay with my wife. I want it to work with her. That sounds sentimental, doesn't it. Did you know I was so sentimental?"

Then I stood up from my chair. And this is what I remember: I walked over to the window and reached out my hand to him. Miraculously, we shook hands. Man to man, both trying to cope in a world of unfathomable emotion, anger, jealousy, and human failing, a world that Karl Jaspers and the existentialists knew well.

"Now," said Galloway, "if you don't mind, can you leave?"

THAT'S the way I've always remembered it. I was angry, although I was not savage. But I should have been savage. I should have wrenched his arm out of its socket.

For years I remembered that meeting with Galloway as a turning point in my maturity. I thought that for the first time I was able to look down on myself from above and see myself on the stage of life. I could have threatened Galloway, but I didn't. I could have physically assaulted him, but I didn't. I listened. I sympathized with him, as despicably as he acted. I understood that the world is made of the head and the heart together, that life is not reasonable but we must still struggle against life. I rose above the situation, like an eagle. For years I believed those things. What was I thinking? All of that bullshit rationalization makes me sick.

And what I prided myself on most was that seemingly magnificent gesture at the end of the encounter, reaching out my hand to him. There was Galloway, twenty-five years older than me, a man of the world, a college professor, a scholar of literature, a man who had been fucking my girlfriend, and it was me, not him, who extended his hand. Because I believed that I understood what he was saying. I believed: to reach out my hand like that, I must have understood. I must have understood that there was some kind of bond between us. What nauseating bullshit. My hand will always be dirty.

Sometimes I wonder how Galloway remembers that morning so many years ago. Or if he remembers it at all. He would be well into his seventies now, perhaps he's no longer alive. For a few years I kept track of him, drawn to him the way one is drawn to the people one hates. I heard that he divorced his wife and left the college, moved, and joined the faculty of some prep school on the West Coast. Then moved again. About fifteen years ago I saw the name James Galloway listed as one of the judges for a college poetry contest, but I didn't know whether it was the same Galloway. Once I admired him. Wouldn't he be pleased to see how faithfully I've followed in his footsteps.

I wish I could talk to him just about that one meeting. Did I threaten him or not?

Did I reach out my hand to him or not?

ON his midnight walk home from the library, Charles comes upon the jumpy light of a bonfire, another late-night Vietnam War protest rally. Flickering students chant and wave cardboard placards and pass out pamphlets. "Sign this petition." "Will you help picket the secretary of state on Thursday night?" All very orchestrated and businesslike, quite different from the angry confusion of three months ago.

People get used to anything, he thinks. Another of the incomprehensibles. He wonders if he will get used to Juliana's betrayal. Even now, weeks later, she will not talk to him about Galloway and acts as if she did nothing wrong. Snaps at him for interfering with her life. "You don't control me," she said.

Were this a poker game, she would have outplayed him easily. If she loved him, as she says she does, she would talk to him about her mother, she would discuss their future together, she would explain why she began sleeping with Galloway. Instead she lies in his arms in the ballerinas' dressing room and asks him to recite poetry to her. And he does, although the poems now seem brittle and dark. Whatever she asks. He stitches the small tears in her leotards. He helps her work through the contract for her upcoming performances in May. He sponges her body when she is too tired to move. Whatever she asks. With each passing day he loves her more.

Imprisoned. He is a prisoner to her. He tries to imagine her ten years from now: beginning to gain weight, lines of frustration and defeat showing in her face, teaching ballet classes to young girls in a room filled with mirrors and brass barres. Or perhaps the lucky break, the anointment from Balanchine.

A cold wind tears through his clothing. Shivering, he stands near the fire. Its heat melts the snow in a wide circle of slush and mud. He sees people he knows: Phillipe Renault, Fred Morgan, his roommate from freshman year,

Robby Talbot, a quiet boy who draws imaginary maps on his wall. Standing on a Coca-Cola crate, one of the students is reading a speech through a bullhorn. Dormitory windows open, people yell into the frigid night to be quiet. Go to bed.

Yes, go to bed. He should go to bed, lie in his easy soft bed. Suddenly he feels like a coward. Going to the war, or refusing to go, would take courage. He simply drifts. Wayne Manning joined the Black Panthers last month after a shootout at UCLA. David Lassal left for Biafra to work for the World Food Program. And he, stumbling on to this careful protest rally, just returned from his cozy desk in the library, where he was studying poetry and the architecture of Islamic Spain and Plato's *Republic*. He is a coward. He wants to risk himself for something he believes in and at the same time doesn't know what he believes in. Except Juliana.

Who else is here at this polite protest rally? He wants to wrestle someone to the mud, break bones.

"Charles."

He looks up to see Ralph, holding a placard and a tennis ball can filled with beer. Ralph's placard, in neat stenciled letters, says "America Get Out." In recent months Ralph has demonstrated an excessive capacity for scholarship. For his senior paper he is doggedly pursuing an unknown eighteenth-century British botanist named Stephen

Lithgrave who, according to Ralph, devised a classification system for plants well in advance of Linnaeus. Every week Ralph brings Charles drawings, convoluted diagrams, garden journals. Charles feels affection for Ralph. Ralph is also a coward, but an enthusiastic coward. For his part Charles has abandoned his paper on Emily Dickinson. He couldn't possibly tolerate supervisory meetings with Galloway. Yet he still attends Galloway's lectures and finds a shameful pleasure in reminding Galloway, through his mere presence, that he is the victor, that it is he who finally gets the girl.

"How's the self?" says Ralph. "Still doing the deed with the little ballerina?"

"Please don't talk about her like that."

"Pardon moi, the faux pas." Ralph grins, showing the perfect teeth that have been straightened at great cost to his parents. "Lighten up. This is a protest rally."

Ralph tosses his collection of protest pamphlets into the fire. Other students are feeding the bonfire with second-hand furniture from their rooms, clothing, shoes, notebooks. The fire groans and belches like a gassy old man.

"Listen," Charles says, "don't you have a cousin or somebody who works at Saks Fifth Avenue in New York?"

"Uncle."

"Okay, uncle. Could you do me a favor?"

Ralph tightens the belt of his dark green army trench-coat. "Sure, just name it."

"Could you ask your uncle if he can find a job in the store for Juliana? She's working in this crappy restaurant."

Ralph whistles. "I have to call him up? What would Juliana do at Saks Fifth Avenue?"

"She could do anything. She could sell clothes. Or jewelry."

"So, she would be a salesman." He pronounces the words slowly, like a child who has never heard them before. "What experience does she have selling clothes?"

"Experience? People learn how to sell clothes." He is irritated by Ralph's plodding, correct questions, as if he were the boss assigning the job. Talking to him is like trying to lift a suitcase full of cement. "Juliana has a head on her shoulders. You've met her. She can learn how to sell anything. Come on, Ralph."

"Why can't she keep her job at the restaurant?"

"She can keep her job at the restaurant. But it's killing her. She hates her job."

Ralph shakes his head. "I don't know. I'm not good at this stuff. I can't even get a job for myself. I'll have to think about it."

———

Two campus police officers have arrived, carrying billy clubs. They are sympathetic to the protesters but must do their duty. "Go to bed, guys." Smell of marijuana in the air. The officers stagger about, pretending they are stoned too, then gently herd the students to their dormitories.

Charles cannot sleep. He feels that he is in a steel box whose walls are moving closer and closer on all sides. Closing his eyes tightly, he sees her dancing, floating through pure air. He lives from one visit with her to the next.

On Monday she calls him from Frankie's. "I've missed my period," she says.

He mumbles into the telephone, trying to understand what she has said. "Could it be the BZ?" he asks.

"No. I've been taking BZ two years, and I've never missed before."

"When was it supposed to be?"

"On Wednesday. I'm very regular. I'm going crazy."

"Give it a few more days." He doesn't know what he's saying. He wants to reassure her. If he could touch her, he could reassure her.

"I'm going crazy, Charles. I can't get pregnant."

In the background he hears the rattle of glasses, talking and laughing. "You're not pregnant," he says. "Missing one period doesn't make you pregnant." Don't women have false alarms about these things all the time? She sounds hysterical. "I'll meet you at the studio tomorrow afternoon," he says. "Okay?"

"What?"

"I'll meet you at the studio tomorrow afternoon. I'll cut my afternoon classes."

"Okay. Okay."

When he arrives at the studio, just at the break between sessions, she does something that she's never done before: she runs to him, in front of everyone, and throws her arms around him. "You're here, you're here, you're here," she whispers. He can feel her heart beating against his chest. She will not let go of him. "I couldn't be pregnant," she whispers. "I couldn't be." Somewhere other dancers are talking quietly and making their shuffling sounds as they exercise. Juliana leans in to him, gives him her weight. "I couldn't be."

"No." He holds her tightly and smells the lavender mixed with sweat. With dusk coming, the air in the studio is thick, like water. Sounds seem magnified. The pianist, off duty, begins playing an arrangement of "Yesterday," lovely and haunting. "No, you aren't pregnant."

Still embracing him, she whispers: "I'm glad you came. It's a long trip, isn't it."

REUNION

He has brought a present for her. Hand in hand they walk to the back corridor, where he opens the small box and takes out the silver bracelet with amber stones. He places it around her wrist, a silver moon crescent against a pink sky.

"You shouldn't give me so many presents," she says. Then she kisses him, and he is happy that the hysteria is over. He wants her the way she was, before Galloway.

TWELVE

THAT night he doesn't stay with her but takes the late bus back to his college. It is a gruesome trip, in the middle of the night, and he would much rather spend the dark hours in her arms, but he has missed too many classes, and he has already made plans to see her on Saturday. For some reason he feels that he has demonstrated his love more forcefully by not staying, by not asking anything from her in return. Just making the trip to comfort her and then leaving. He has forgiven her affair with Galloway. Unconditional love. That's what he wants to give her and what he wants from her. People should give without wanting anything in return. All other giving is selfish. But he is being selfish a little, isn't he, by wanting her to love him in return? He hopes that she loves him in return. Is it possible for a person to love without wanting love back? Is anything so pure? Or is love, by its nature, a reciprocity, like oceans and clouds, an evaporating of seawater and a replenishing by rain? As he contemplates these questions, with the beams of passing vehicles sweeping one after another through the dark, silent bus, his head sinks against the hard metal seat and he drifts into sleep.

At one in the morning, the bus pulls wheezing and snorting into the little station near the college. The station is freezing and smells of spilled beer and worse. There is a dirty linoleum floor, a calendar on the wall flipped to the month of June, an overhead fluorescent bulb, broken and flickering like a Christmas tree light. Two men in raggedy overcoats, with socks for gloves, sit shuddering on a bench. Is this place real? Each object and each person seems to vanish in Charles's memory as soon as he looks away, like disappearing ink. He hurries out of the station, crosses the street, and enters the campus. On each side of the walkway, a wall of snow. Sleep.

"HERE we see a northern view of the Patio de Comares of the Alhambra, built by Ismail I, continued by Yusuf I, and completed by his son Muhammad V in 1370. Note the central arch with three smaller arches on each side, the delicately carved woodwork above each arch, so much in contrast to the solid, mountainlike stone wall rising above and behind, as if we are meant to feel both the art and the might of Islam at once. The reflecting pool and its marble border guide the eye to the central arch. Inside is a maze of interlocking courtyards, each accommodating particular bureaucracies."

Has he heard his professor's words or dreamed them? He is half asleep, imagining that he and Juliana are making love on the sultan's cushion in the inner court of the Patio de Comares. It is a velvet cushion of deep purple and gold, as long as a human body.

The professor is a tight little man with a tight little mustache. He wears a gray suit, perfectly fitted around his nervous shoulders, a club pin of some kind in his lapel. When he paces, the silver chain of his pocketwatch jingles against his hip. Now, as he advances his projector to the next slide, he hesitates and gazes at Charles in the dim light, as if asking him to watch carefully. He admires Charles's poetic descriptions of the architecture of Islamic Spain, admires them so much that he uses them himself in his lectures, he has used them today. In fact, he has quietly asked Charles to collaborate with him on his next book.

In the darkened classroom Charles drowsily slumps at his desk, aware of the professor's entreating gaze. Other students also drowsily slump at their desks, some of them even snore. But the professor is not gazing at them. Charles looks up at the white shimmer of screen and feels something hovering.

ON Saturday she is sick. She vomits during her morning class. Asks him to leave, then asks him to stay, then leave again. She trudges to the bathroom, changes out of her stained leotard, and returns wearing one of his long-sleeved white shirts, loosely hanging over her denim jeans.

"Let me come with you to your aunt's," he says. "I'll rub your forehead with cool water."

"No," she says. "Kik will take care of me."

"Please," he says. He tries to embrace her.

"Don't. Don't look at me. I look terrible."

"You're just sick. Everybody gets sick. I want to take care of you." Class has resumed. Dancers bend and flex to the barking orders of the dominatrix.

"I have to leave," she says, moving toward the door. "The piano is pounding my head. Please don't come with me. You are so sweet. I'll call you tomorrow. I'll be fine by tomorrow."

Next week her nausea goes away for a few days and then returns. When he meets her at Frankie's late Wednesday night, she is so fatigued that she can barely stand on her feet. How did she possibly work for six hours? In the subway car she leans against him and falls asleep on his shoulder. Tonight he will just take her home. At the doorstep of her aunt's apartment, he asks her to see a doctor. No, she says, she will not see a doctor. When would she have time to see a doctor? At least stop working at Frankie's for a few days, he suggests. That's impossible, she says. In the bright light of the lamp above her aunt's door, she seems pale and drained. Is there a chance she could be pregnant? he asks. She can't get pregnant, she answers. She's not pregnant, she just has the flu. Feed a cold and starve the flu. She's eating too much, she says. Starve the flu.

A week later she calls him, late. Her voice is thin paper. "Guess what," she says, "I'm not pregnant."

"How do you know? Did you go to a doctor?"

"No. But I've lost weight. I'm 102. When you're pregnant, you gain weight. I knew that I wasn't pregnant."

"How are you feeling?"

She begins crying.

"Juliana. What is it?"

"I don't know. I feel so sad. I don't know why."

"Juliana, please see a doctor." He can barely hear her against the noise of the restaurant.

"Talk to me. Why do I feel like this?"

"Please see a doctor. Whatever it is, we'll handle it. Please go see a doctor."

"Okay. They're calling me now," she says between sobs. "I've got to go. Come next Tuesday."

THEY sit on the cot of the ballerinas' dressing room, eating slices of an apple.

"Where did you get it?" she asks.

"Some grocery store. I have more. It's a Macintosh, isn't it?"

"I don't know. I don't know the names of things. You're much better at that." Slowly she peels away the red skin with her fingernail. She is eating. With the apple, she swallows two little blue pills and takes a drink from her thermos. She's thinner than he's ever seen her.

As they eat slices of apple, they listen to the slow drip of the sink faucet. Her clothes lie in a heap on the wet floor, and she wears only the turquoise silk robe that he has given her. The last slice of apple.

"Tell me," he says.

"I'm pregnant."

"Pregnant." He repeats the word as if it were any other word. It is still only a word, isn't it? The word echoes and echoes and echoes.

"The doctor says that I'm between six and seven weeks. That's why I've been sick. I'm pregnant."

He is still hearing the echo of the word. Has he known all along that she was pregnant? That he has done this thing to her?

"I'm going to get an abortion," she says. She begins crying. The tears slide down her face and her neck. "Lynn has a doctor who can do it for $450. I don't know where I'll find the money." She pauses and wipes her face with the back of her hand. "Kik is so angry she won't talk to me about it."

His mind is reeling. He needs to think. "I'll help you pay for it. I'll pay for it."

She ties a knot in the silk sash of her robe, unties it, ties it again. She is not looking at him. "I'll pay you back in six months," she says.

"You don't need to pay me back. This is my problem too."

"But I want to pay you back. I won't take the money unless you let me pay you back."

He nods. Never has she asked him for anything before, and he knows that she hates asking him for money. He looks at the long curve of her neck, the slenderness of her, and he tries to imagine her stomach expanding, bigger and bigger, her flowerlike breasts growing heavy and thick. A baby inside of her. His baby.

"I have to do it in the next month," she says. "My dancing, it's very bad for my dancing being pregnant, you know. I'm not dancing well. I'm dancing like shit. Our performances start at the beginning of May. That's two months from now."

He gives her the corner of his shirt to dab the tears. "Yes, you're right. You have to get an abortion soon. I'll go with you. I'll talk to the doctor."

She buries her head in his shoulder. He can feel her shaking. "Lynn told me that sometimes when you have an abortion, you can't have children again. Do you think that's true?"

"I don't know," he says. "No, I don't think that could be true. Maybe in rare cases. You'll have children."

"I've got to have an abortion."

"Yes." He wants to help her, he loves her more than ever, and yet he also wants to escape, escape her, escape this little room, run down the stone steps to the freezing air. "I'll help. Anything."

The cot moves against the counter, a bottle topples and

falls to the floor, doesn't break but rolls slowly across the warped wooden planks.

"I'm not ready to be a father either," he says. "I have to finish college. I have to get a job. I want to get a job. For us."

"For us? I don't need you to support me." Suddenly she seems angry with him. "You might not be the father, you know."

"What?"

"Jim could be the father. Or you."

"Jim?"

"James Galloway."

"Why did you tell me that?" he shouts.

"I shouldn't have said anything."

"He's a filthy pig. Professor Galloway couldn't be the father. I'm the father."

"What difference does it make who the father is?" she says, standing and swaying on her feet. "I'm getting an abortion."

THE middle of March. He and Ralph poke the milky ice on Celebration Pond to watch it crack and fissure into a dozen islands of glass, each bobbing in the gelid water below. Thinner patches thaw and melt in the sun. With one hand he reaches underneath the slush and pulls out a seed-pod, miraculous, tawny in color, the size of a coffee bean, with a leathery skin and fragile indentations. He splits open the pod, releasing a fine yellow powder that billows and puffs like a tiny sandstorm. How did such softness sleep safe through the winter? Like his child, sleeping in her womb.

That evening his hands are still mustard-colored when he holds the framed photograph of Juliana on his desk. She balances on the toes of one foot, her heel arched. Legs form a perfect right angle, one straight up and down and the other an arrow shot from the hip. Her arms float. Her hands and fingers open and reach out as delicately as if she were plucking the strings of a harp made of air. Air, mare, fair, take me to your lair. Her straw-colored hair is tied back in a bun, and she stares directly at the camera with a gentle concentration. Can she see him looking at her in the photograph? In his mind he hears her softly whispering: Dance with me. Go up and go up. I am your body. Your poem is my blood. Go up and go up. I am your body, your poem is my blood.

After all that has happened, she remains his beauty, his purity, his clarity. When the abortion is over, he will talk to her again about the years ahead. He wants to take her away from her terrible aunt, live with her in an apartment that looks out on a small park. Each morning they will wake up in each other's arms, he will brush her hair and fasten it with the silky gold ribbons that she likes. Can she hear him? He pushes his finger hard against the sharp metal edge of the frame, cuts through the skin, and drips a few drops of blood onto the glass. Can she feel the red blood? The future enters him.

HE massages her legs. It seems that he's been massaging her legs for hours. Back and forth, back and forth, waves rolling one after another. What day is it? He hardly knows where he is. Back and forth. Billie Holiday softly sings on the cracked radio by the cot.

She suddenly sits up, the oil glistening on her legs in the dim light of the lamp. "I have to go to class," she says. "I'll be late for class."

Sleepily he looks at his watch. "It's three in the morning."

"Then I have to do my stretches." She stands up, takes off her silk robe, and begins deep knee bends. The air in the room, musty and still from having been enclosed for hours, seems to cling to her body.

"What are you doing?"

"I'm doing my stretches. I've been dancing like triple shit."

"Juliana. It's three in the morning. Please. You need to rest."

"I need to do my stretches." She goes down and up. The wood floor creaks with each repetition. With her arms on the counter, she raises a leg, horizontal but limp, and lets it drop. She's exhausted.

"Juliana. Please." He holds her. She struggles against him.

"Stay away from me," she says.

"Juliana." She's wrecking herself right in front of him. He must help her. "Juliana, please. Please lie down and rest. You need rest."

"I've got to do my stretches. I've got to be light."

He hates the ballet. He hates the pregnancy. For a moment the radio goes silent, then Billie Holiday begins singing again, slow and sad. Juliana's back is dimpled from the canvas of the cot. He puts his arms around her again, trying to make her lie down, but she pulls away from him. Her hair falls stringy and wild to her shoulders.

"Charles," she says. She stops her exercises. "Charles. I want to ask you something. Okay?" She stares at him, waiting.

"Okay."

"Do you think I'm pretty?"

Tears form in his eyes. "Yes."

A WEEK before the scheduled abortion, they have an appointment with the doctor. His office is in a small clinic not far from the Magay studio, a three-story brick building with one ambulance parked quietly under a tree.

"I'm glad both of you came," says the doctor. He is a heavy blond man in his forties. He smiles, almost with embarrassment. "It's not often that the fellow comes along." He takes out a clipboard, studies it for a moment, then turns to Juliana. "You've had your talk with Miss Noyes?" Juliana nods. The doctor holds her in his gaze, pleasant but like a steel beam. "And this is something you want to do? You've thought about it?"

"Yes." Her voice sounds as if it has come from the far side of the moon.

Charles grips her hand, presses himself against her on the small sofa. He wants to comfort her, yet he himself feels as if he could vomit. It is too warm. Somewhere a heating vent is blasting hot air into the room. He has begun to sweat, he can feel the wet in his armpits. He takes off his jacket. Still the heat swarms around him. Why is he here?

This sweaty cage of a room, the overly kind doctor. He turns to look at Juliana. Is she thinking about the abortion? Or her aunt's fury? Or how she will dance in tomorrow's rehearsal? He has noticed that her stomach is just beginning to curve. She has noticed.

"You're sure?" says the doctor.

"What?"

"You're sure you want this abortion?"

"Yes," she says, this time loudly. "What kind of question is that? I can't possibly have a baby now. I'm a dancer. I have rehearsals and performances."

"I'll bet you're a wonderful dancer," says the doctor.

"She is," says Charles. He leans over and kisses her, sweaty.

The doctor waits. He continues staring at her with his steel-beam eyes. Why does he keep staring?

"Can't you see that she's sure?" demands Charles.

"Okay," says the doctor. He explains the procedure. As the doctor describes cervical canals and dilations and the scraping of tissues, Charles feels the room spinning around him.

"I have to go over only one more thing," says the doctor. Quickly he glances at the clock on his desk. "Do you want to be completely unconscious? We can work with a local anesthetic that will leave you awake."

"I don't know," says Juliana. She turns to Charles. "I can't think."

"It's up to you," says the doctor.

She puts her hands to her face. "I don't know. I don't care." The doctor nods. She lets out a long breath. "Will I be able to have children? Later?"

"There is every probability."

THAT week he runs into Professor Galloway in the student-faculty lounge. Galloway sits alone at a table, reading, his boots propped up on the neighboring chair as if he owns the place. From across the room Charles spots him and hesitates. Does he know that Juliana is pregnant? Charles feels both revulsion and attraction for Galloway. He is an amoral, arrogant man. At the same time, he and Charles have shared . . . What have they shared? A secret place. What does that make them? Something that has no name.

In his haughtiness and eternal suffering, Galloway has no children. Will never have children. The closest he will ever come to fatherhood is this fleeting pregnancy, to be sloughed in a few days. For an instant Charles has the urge to tell Galloway about the pregnancy, make him believe that he is the father, that he almost had a child but not quite. Stab him.

Galloway turns the page of his newspaper, looks up, and sees Charles across the room.

"Charles."

Against his will, Charles finds himself walking to Galloway's table. Tell him. Stab him.

"How is it with Juliana?" Galloway asks in a low, confidential voice. "Are you still seeing each other?"

What game is he playing? Charles wonders. "It's extremely good with Juliana," he says. But that isn't enough, that won't wound him nearly enough. Should he tell him? He wonders if Galloway has already found some other young woman to pump blood into his body. For a horrifying moment he has the sensation of trading places with his professor, of being forty-five years old himself, in the middle of his life, sitting with his newspaper and talking to a young student.

"Juliana wants me to marry her," Charles blurts out.

"Really?" says Galloway. He hesitates. "Is she eating enough? Is she . . ." He doesn't finish the sentence, and Charles says nothing. With a sigh, Galloway folds up his newspaper and places it in his briefcase. "I wanted to tell you one thing," he says. "Because I admire your ferocity. One thing. There will be many women after her. Twenty-five years from now, you may not even remember her name."

"I will," Charles shouts, stupidly. He feels like a child. And he has not said what he wants to say. But the moment has gotten away from him. Galloway rises from his chair, with his halo of sadness, and leaves.

THE next morning Charles wakes up with a clenched jaw. The future has tilted and seethed in his sleep. Everything is wrong. Blind.

He wants the baby.

The certainty of it lies like a bull's-eye painted on his heart. And there at his desk, the photograph of Juliana in her leotard, gazing straight at him. At last he knows where she stares. Accusingly. The baby will stop her dancing for a year. Odd, the voice in his head. He hears the voice talking about "the baby" as if it already exists. Another voice: No, the baby does not yet exist. A baby would end her dancing for a year, maybe longer. How could he wish for that? She must have the abortion.

He wants the baby. The thought shocks him, makes him realize that he doesn't know himself. How could he be so selfish? Can a person forget a desire once it has lived? Or set it on fire?

This morning he cannot bear his roommates. They talk and joke, they toss their books onto the sofa, they play records, they eat doughnuts brought back from the cafeteria. He lives in another universe. If he opened his mouth, no sound would come out. He wants the baby. Why, he doesn't know. He knows only that the baby will murder Juliana.

The gymnasium. How did he get here? Sweat runs down his bare arms and drops very slowly on the lacquered wood floor. The four walls like a neat gift box. He smashes a squash ball against a wall, and it comes back at him, a hard black bullet. He swings and misses. He smashes the ball on the next rebound. What should he do? What can he do? He is ashamed.

THE telephone call to Juliana: We have to talk. In person. I'll see you at the studio. We won't have privacy. Then we'll go outside on the fire-escape landing. I'll meet you at the studio.

When he sees her, he is shaking.

He says: "I want you to have the baby."

"What are you talking about?" She has been dancing, and her face and arms shine.

"I heard our child speaking to me last night in a dream." He grips the metal rail of the landing. "I want to have the baby. I've changed my mind. I'll do anything. I'll quit school. College doesn't mean anything to me. I'll get a job right away. I want us to be a family."

"Charles?" she screams. "You've flipped out. You know that I can't have a baby." Without a coat, she is shivering. Goose bumps appear on her bare arms and shoulders.

"Yes you can. I want this. I know that it's my baby. I'm certain." His eyes become moist. "I want to have it. I'll take care of the child myself if I have to. If you don't want it. I'll take care of the child by myself."

"You can't take care of a baby. You don't know what you're talking about."

"Please, Juliana. Please. I've never felt so certain about anything in my life. For the first time I feel certain about something. I know this."

"What about me?" Juliana begins shouting. "You're just talking about what you want. I can't have a baby. I'm a dancer. You've never really understood that. I'm not giving up my dancing for anything. Why are you doing this to me?"

Her words are so right that he actually hears them a second before she says them. His words. For a moment he is struck dumb to hear his words coming out of her mouth, as if he were a ventriloquist. Yes, she is right. Why is he doing this to her?

"I do understand," he says. He chokes and begins coughing. "Your dancing, I know. I hate asking you this. I hate myself for asking you this. I shouldn't have come here." She stares at him in disbelief. Then he hears himself talking again. "Please. This is my baby. Our baby." He grips her by the wrists. "I am thinking about us. I want us to be a family. I know that you want the baby too."

"I do not want this baby." She bursts into tears. "I do not want the baby. I can't have a baby now. Don't tell me what I want."

"I'm begging you."

She takes a wild swing at him, then rushes back into the building. The heavy fire-escape door clunks shut. For a few moments her smell is still on the landing. He inhales her. He looks over the railing and down, where he sees an alley, a row of garbage cans, a rusting car on cement blocks, a ribbon of blue smoke curling out of a pipe.

THAT night she calls him just as he's falling asleep. "I won't have the abortion," she says.

"What?" He can hardly believe what he's heard. "Do you swear it?"

"Yes." Her voice is a rage. He doesn't know this voice.

And he hears another voice, the aunt shrieking. "I'll never dance again," Juliana screams into the telephone.

"Juliana."

"You've gotten what you want."

"I'll be a good father," he says.

She hangs up.

THIRTEEN

AFTER she hung up, I tried to call her back. I telephoned her aunt's apartment, where I'd never called before, risking the aunt's genteel wrath. The phone rang and rang. For the rest of the night, I walked the campus, praying that she would forgive me.

Now I'm having trouble remembering. I wandered around the campus, yes, I think so. Vaguely I recall dark paths, dark buildings. I can't imagine how I thought I could be a father at that age. I could barely take care of myself. For years I had lived only on my allowance from home. Could I really have heard the unborn child speaking to me?

Was I ready to throw away my college degree in the last se-mester? I am amazed. I had so much power.

Even now I don't know why I suddenly decided that I wanted the baby. That encounter with Galloway the day before . . . good God, could I have been only reacting to that, wanting the baby only to spite Galloway? I can still remember his dismissive look, the way that he folded his newspaper. I know that the uncertainty of the father's iden-tity, at least in Juliana's mind, was a demon in me.

What I wanted, I think, was an anchor. I was confused about everything in my life, and the baby was some kind of anchor in my confusion. A little me, to force some meaning and courage into my life. Can anyone blame me for that? So, I asked her to have the baby. And I wanted the baby for me, not for Juliana and me. No, that's not true. I wanted the baby for both of us. We were in love.

Did Juliana shout when we met that day? I believe I'm the one who shouted. But not on the fire-escape landing. We didn't have our confrontation there. We met in some empty room in the building. I seem to recall a small storage room of some kind with shelves, curling ballet posters on the wall, chairs piled on top of one another for an upcom-ing performance.

I had just arrived from the bus, wild with my decision, wild with my guilt. Against all that was holy, she interrupted a rehearsal in progress. What was she wearing? I want to remember this. I remember a leotard, V-necked against her chest, bare arms and shoulders, slippers I think. Possibly her new leotard, but she went through leotards every couple of months trying to find one that made her feel light enough. When she came to me, she radiated some of the sweaty oblivion that she always had when she danced, but underneath I could see the dread. She was pushing her body far beyond where it should go, even for a dancer, even for someone who habitually leaps and spins on feet ripped and bleeding. And she was acutely aware of the slightest diminution from her top form. At this point she was a knife beginning to dull, and she knew it.

Because the ballerinas' dressing room was being used for the rehearsal, we found the storage room down the corridor.

"I want to have the baby," I said as soon as we were alone.

"What are you talking about?" She looked at me incredulously. As I remember, there was no love in that look, only anger. In a few days she was to be rid of the thing in her uterus, the frictional drag against her high leaps and turns, and I was suddenly standing in her way.

"I want the baby," I repeated.

"Charles! Don't you think this is my decision?"

"It's my decision too," I said. "I'm the father. The father has rights too. I've thought about this, and I've changed my mind. I won't ask you to do anything after the child is born. I'll take care of the child. I'll get any job that I have to." She stared at me. Both of us knew that what I was saying was ridiculous. At least I should have known. "Please listen to me, Juliana," I said. "You want the baby too, I know you do."

Then she started to cry. I can see the dark eyeliner smudging and running down the side of her face. Crying, she was still beautiful.

"Don't do this to me, Charles."

Don't do this to me? Juliana had never before acknowledged that I had any power over her.

Why was she crying? Perhaps she was crying to soften me, to break my resolve, so that in the end she could have the abortion and get on with her dancing life. No, I don't believe that anymore. I think that she loved me. And I believe that some piece of her really did want the baby. She was at war with herself. But I did feel guilty. I did know that a baby would destroy her dancing career.

I put my arms around her and kissed her. I loved her. My love had not lessened a degree. And I found her more sexually attractive than ever. The perspiration mixed with perfume. Her face flushed from dancing and the emotional intensity of the moment. The thin shoulder straps of her leotard, the thin, tightly stretched fabric of the leotard cupping her small breasts, puckered around her nipples. Even the minute curve of her belly. I wanted to make love to her there, in the storage room, that instant.

"I can't have the baby," she cried out and pushed me away. "I can't have the baby. You're a selfish bastard. You're like every other man. I thought you were different. You only think about yourself."

"Who is the selfish one?" I shouted. But thinking back on it now, I don't think I said that. And I don't think she said it either. There was no selfishness in our relationship, at least no more than the usual selfishness of a person trying to live in the world. We loved each other. Don't people give up some of themselves when they love? I think I wanted the baby for my anchor, and for us. She wanted her dancing because that was the life that she knew, the way she had escaped her alcoholic mother, her passion. She did have a passion, and I envied her for it. Maybe that's why I wanted the baby. Did I understand these things at the time? Did we know that we were tearing our little paper universe into shreds? Too late.

Weeping, she ran from the room, down the hallway, and disappeared.

REUNION

————

SOMEONE is calling to him from far away, a voice he recognizes but doesn't recognize. Is it her? No, it's his mother. She's telling him something about the baby, and he's straining to hear what she says.

He's been dreaming. He sits up in his dormitory bed, stiff, still wearing his clothes from last night, like a costume from a nightmarish Halloween party. It's afternoon. Aretha Franklin wails from the next room. Sleepily he picks up the telephone and leaves a message at the Magay studio for her to call him at the next break. He'll wait by the telephone.

He has a headache. He sits by the telephone, tries to read one of his textbooks, and feels like he is swimming in oil. The same paragraph, over and over. Puts the book down and stares at an ant slowly crossing the table. It is a black ant. Every few seconds it halts, its tiny elbowed antennae wave and search in the air, its mandibles open and close as if crushing a victim. Then the crawling again. It drags its oval abdomen behind like a slave carrying a burden. He watches as the ant painstakingly makes its long journey across the table, stopping and starting, jaws opening and shutting. How odd, he thinks, his watching these seconds in the life of this ant.

You are too sweet to me. It is Juliana's voice in his head.

Once he sucked the blood from a cut on her hand. He waits.

That night he telephones Frankie's. "She's stepped out for a few minutes," someone says to him. In an hour he leaves another message. No one answers the telephone at the aunt's apartment.

He decides to give her a few days to calm down, and him.

What can he do to begin preparing for fatherhood? None of his friends are fathers. Some of the graduate students are fathers. Occasionally he sees them walking across campus with their children, the toddlers running a few steps and then tumbling on the grass, strollers for the babies, backpacks spilling diapers and bottles and a trail of small plastic toys. Now he tries to imagine himself. This is how you giggle at a baby. This is how you hold a baby: with a hand supporting the head and neck. Chubby cheeks and Juliana's green eyes. Already he loves the child. Can he love the child when he knows what it has cost its mother?

I'm going to be a father, he tells Ralph as they cross the diagonal path. Ralph whistles. No shit. Was it an accident? No accident, says Charles. We've decided to have a baby together. Ralph whistles again. I had no idea you guys were that serious. Wow. Congratulations, I guess. That's serious shit.

Juliana, forgive me, he thinks. She will forgive him. She wants the baby too. She can dance again as soon as the baby is born. He will do all that he can to help her dance. Juliana, I'll be a good father. Whenever he is alone, he finds himself talking to her.

On Friday, four days of silence, time enough. His nerves are taut wires. He skips his late-morning classes, takes the bus to New York, the subway to the East Village, the three flights of stone steps to the dance studio. Rehearsal is in session.

But she's not there. He feels like a stranger, as if he has accidentally stumbled into this cavernous room with the high ceilings and windows and barres. Maddeningly, the piano plays. Why does the piano play when she is not here?

Grace ceases her pliés as soon as she sees him. "Juliana stopped coming to rehearsal three days ago," she says. "We've been unable to reach her. Do you know where she is?"

"No," he says. "I thought she would be here." Somewhere he knew that she would not be here, a vast black knowing like a black lake. The lake pours foul into his stomach.

Grace wipes her face with a Kleenex. "This is so unlike her. We're worried that something's happened. She hasn't been herself for the last month or two. Well, you know that." She looks at him with embarrassment. "Is she pregnant?" She hesitates. "I'm sorry if I've said something wrong."

He closes his eyes. What should he say? "Yes."

"I see," says Grace. "We weren't sure. We thought so."

The piano stops. People move around him, shapes. He leans against the wall. Did she have the abortion after all? Could she be extremely ill? Why hasn't she returned his calls? People are talking to him, voices underwater. Sound and light are flattened out.

"I don't know where she is," someone whispers to him. It's Lynn. "Honest. She called me yesterday, long distance. She's gone off somewhere with her aunt. It's a shock. She wouldn't tell me where."

"What?" He looks up to see Lynn's face near his, her mouth. "What? She's gone? I don't believe you."

"Honest. Will you tell me if you find her? I thought she was getting an abortion. I thought that's why she didn't show up. Do you think she'll come back?"

HE runs down the stone steps and flags a taxi to the aunt's apartment. Cars jerk past like flailing animals.

How dead the apartment seems. He knocks at the door for five minutes, continues knocking until neighbors shout at him to stop. There should be some security in this place, someone yells. Then the supervisor is standing behind him, hairy and fat in his undershirt. They've left, says the supervisor, the girl and her aunt. Left two days ago. Packed up the place in one day, like thieves, a truck was here and then gone. Gave two months' rent, in cash, and left without any forwarding address. The girl was a fine piece, says the supervisor, winking, young but legal. Charles could crush him.

"Where did they go?" he asks numbly.

"Hell if I know," says the supervisor. "Left like thieves in the night." A thick clutch of keys dangles from his belt.

"Can I go in?" asks Charles. "Just for ten minutes?"

"Nope," says the supervisor.

Charles peers through the glass peephole and sees the small sitting room, empty except for the sofa table. Metal hangers and crumpled newspapers litter the floor. And beyond the sitting room, a tiny hallway, two doors opening to two rooms. All of it grotesquely curved and warped through the lens of the peephole, like the farcical image of a person in the wavy mirror at an amusement park.

Without any plan, he hails another taxi back to the Magay studio. It's a quarter past five, just after finishing, but the door hasn't yet been locked. In a daze he walks through the studio, past moving people, to the ballerinas' dressing room.

Her counter. The mirror. The sink. He picks up the sponge at the sink and holds it against his face. The cot. He sits on the cot, he leans down and smells the canvas where her body has been.

After a period of time, he doesn't know how long, Lynn comes into the room. He looks up to see her there in tight jeans, a tight sweater, barefoot. She closes the door behind her.

"I hope you don't mind," she whispers. When he says nothing, she sits down beside him on the cot. He doesn't want her here. She leans back against the wall, the cot shifts. "I know that you and Juliana came here," she says. She puts her hand on his hand. "I would have come here with you. I would still. Do you think I'm terrible?"

In his mind he is still back at the aunt's apartment, the awful desolation of it through the peephole. Where has Juliana gone? Has she fled from him because of love or because of hate? It has to be one or the other. He looks down and discovers Lynn's hand, white. Against his will, he finds himself attracted to her. Leave me, he thinks. He cannot move.

"Are you the father?" Lynn asks. "Of Juliana's baby?"

"I don't know," he says lifelessly. "I think so."

"You want it, don't you. I can tell." She leans her head on his shoulder. "She'll call you. I'm sure she will." She squeezes his hand. "I wonder if she'll have the baby. I can't see Juliana with a baby. But it will be a beautiful baby. Juliana has a beautiful face, doesn't she."

He cannot talk. He knows that this moment is the last moment of a world. This breath is the last breath of a world. He looks up to the ceiling and stares at the hanging silk scarf and notices for the first time, after all these months, a pair of red lips, pursed in a kiss.

I HAVE no words. I who have made my living at words, reading words, teaching words, once writing words. This secret: Words fail.

I've seen war documentaries of soldiers with their heads blown off or their intestines spilling out like coiled sausage or their legs severed clean in the sand. It's like that.

In the October after my graduation, the month when the baby would be coming into the world somewhere, I turned on my radio so loud that I nearly went deaf. I wanted to go deaf. Or blind, but I didn't have the courage for that. When did I have courage?

My child would be nearly thirty now. Is nearly thirty

now. Not a child anymore, but a young man or young woman. A sister or brother to Emily. I have never stopped loving this child I don't know. Sometimes I think that the reason I never gave Emily enough love was because I was holding some back for the other.

I often wonder: Does the child have her dancer's body? Or my wrestler's body? Her eyes or mine? What has Juliana said to our child about me? What does she remember? Sometimes I think: If I've never seen the child, if I've never touched the child, then perhaps the child doesn't really exist. I can imagine the child out of existence. At other times I think: Perhaps I do not need to imagine the child out of existence. Perhaps Juliana never had the baby after all. I don't know which possibility is worse.

My child would be nearly thirty now. Older than I was as I sat on that cot in the ballerinas' dressing room and stared blankly and dead at the red lips. I remember where my hands were, the angle of my head, my breathing. How tender I was. I was a child myself, slaughtered. Who let this happen? Who could let this happen?

NIGHT has descended. Now I can see nothing in this place. The Trustees Room sleeps in complete darkness, except for the small moon of the security light in the corner. It must be nine o'clock, maybe ten. I am stiff from standing here so many hours. I stretch, I scratch my nose. I need to go to the toilet. Outside the leaded glass window, I can see the dark shape of the oak tree. Tents glow in the distance, dark knots of people stumble drunkenly about the grounds. Muffled music from the parties, scattered like small brushfires.

In the darkness, feeling along walls, I wander out of the Trustees Room and out of the building. I am destroyed all over again. I want to lie down, I want to go home. What is this? My hand, shaking. I must ask someone the way to the boathouse. Ralph is there.

Let me think. I'll stay here a few minutes under the oak tree and collect my thoughts. In a few minutes I'll go down to the boathouse.

Someone seems to be standing near the walkway. "Who's there?" I squint in the dim light of the lamppost. A young man, maybe a student. He nods to me. He seems distraught and keeps rubbing his face.

"Did you find her?" he asks.

"Who?"

"Juliana."

I know this young man. After all that has happened these last hours, I am not shocked to see him. "No, I never found her."

Despite the darkness, I think I can see tears in his eyes. Perhaps I am mistaken.

"I searched for her," I say. "I promise. I searched for her and the baby. I talked to everyone I could find who knew her. She never came back to New York. For years I kept querying the ballet companies. I went to Virginia and tried to locate her mother. But it was hopeless, I knew so little of her life. She disappeared."

He is staring at me. "Will I ever see my child?" he asks. "Please."

"I don't think so." He is so tender. He breaks my heart. What can I say to comfort him? "You'll get over Juliana. You'll forget her. You'll forget about the child."

"No I won't," he says. "You're lying. Don't lie to me."

"Okay." My legs buckle beneath me. I must lean against the tree. There my shoulder finds the rough bark. I feel his eyes on me, like a hand.

"You haven't forgotten them, Juliana and the child, have you? Have you? Have you?"

"No," I whisper. I can barely talk. "I think of them every day." He has put his finger on my heart. He is also wiser than I am. I have lost everything.

In the distance I hear a group of guys singing: *Take me back, take me back to that place so dear, To the fields so green and the arches of white, Of those days of fellowship and joy I sing.* For a few moments the singing grows louder and more boisterous. Then the voices diminish to tiny yelps as the men move through the Baston Arch and out into the dark, sloping courtyards of the east campus.

"What was it like to make love to her?" I ask.

"You don't remember?"

"Tell me."

"I can't describe it," he says. But I can see the power of it in his face. The life force, the rush of blood. He has loved, and he has been loved.

"Just tell me about the first time," I say. "What was it like the first time you made love to her?"

"I can't remember," he says.

He must remember. Could his extravagance be that enormous? He burns universes.

But I have done far worse. I have squandered his future. I have stolen what he has and squandered it. And I must tell him, I have to tell him. I should roll in the dirt and tell him. "My life . . ."

"No," he says. "I don't want to know anything more."

"There are things I have to tell you." He must let me talk to him. He is hoping for so much that will never happen.

I begin again, but he holds up his hand. "Don't," he

says. "I don't want to know anything more. I just want to live." He takes a step back, into shadows, and is gone.

I cannot move. I want to go to the boathouse, but I cannot move. I have nothing inside of me. I am empty. Voices. Another singing group passes by in the night, and I listen dumbly as the sounds swell and fade. After a few moments I hear a different sound: my own heavy breathing.

"CHARLES? You're not wearing that to the movies, are you? You look like one of the Three Stooges."

"I wanted to dress properly for your film."

"My film. So now it's my film. It's Jean Doumer's film."

Sheila herself looks beautiful. She's got herself fixed up. She walks over and straightens my tie and gently smooths my hair.

"There," she says. "Now you're a little more presentable." She steps back and smiles at me. "You're getting revenge for my not going with you to your reunion, aren't you. I don't blame you. I should have gone. I hope you'll forgive me."

"Don't worry about it."

"I'll bet you didn't go to a single one of the parties. You misanthrope." She laughs. "But I'm taking you out tonight.

You're going to see *L'habitude* whether you want to or not."

"I won't like it." I've heard about *L'habitude*. It's a pretentious French version of one of Humberside's lesser stories. And I hate seeing movies with subtitles. They remind me of my sixth-grade teacher's red corrections on my school papers.

"I really want you to see this movie. It's gorgeous and sunny and people are dancing. And after the movie we're going out to dinner. I've made reservations at a perfect little place. Now close your eyes. I've got a surprise for you."

I can't imagine what Sheila is talking about. I am going to close my eyes as she asks, but first I want to memorize the room. The maroon silk rug lies slightly askew on the wood floor. On the mantel I see a stack of books, mostly unread, some thick and some thin, like uneven colored bricks. Shelves of more books. The corner chair that I bought years ago with its semicircular back and rush seat. A porcelain lamp. A framed print of a Japanese woman in an ornate kimono. A small couch, half covered in shadow. Overhead silver fan blades revolve in slow motion. I myself am standing near my desk, my arms at my sides, feeling a certain solidness, as if I've settled down into my body. Sheila rests against the glass-paneled door. She wears a sleeveless blue dress with a white collar, dark blue buttons, high heels. I close my eyes.

"You have them closed tight? No peeking."

"My eyes are closed." I hear something rustling. Then her hand against my cheek.

"Keep your eyes closed," she says.

Her hand feels wonderful on my cheek. I reach out, my eyes still closed, and touch her face, her eyelids, her nose, her lips.

"Charles," she whispers. "You're interfering with my surprise. I'll wait until later." She leans in to me. "Maybe we shouldn't go out tonight."

Slowly I move my hand over her face, like a blind man. I've never touched her like this. Keeping my eyes closed, I pull her to me. Sheila, sweet Sheila.

"Charles, are you crying? I've never seen you cry before. What is it, honey? Tell me."

"Hold me."

"Of course I'll hold you. There. I'll hold you all night. I want you to tell me what's the matter."

ACKNOWLEDGMENTS

I am deeply grateful to Richard Colton, dancer and teacher, for introducing me to the world of ballet and for helpful comments on the manuscript. Likewise, I thank Meghan Beals for showing me the Pearl Theater in New York, I thank the Tricia Brown dance corps, the Paul Taylor Dance Studio, and the Royal Ballet—all for letting me attend rehearsals and classes.

For asteroidal and historical astronomical facts, I thank Brian Marsden, Gareth Williams, and Chuck Whitney.

For help with military matters, I thank Steve Xenakis.

For helpful comments on the manuscript, I thank Isabelle De Courtivron, Michael Rothschild, and LaRose Coffey.

As always, I am indebted to the editorial guidance of my editor Dan Frank, and to the encouragement of my literary agent Jane Gelfman.

Finally, I thank my family, Jean, Elyse, and Kara, for their helpful comments on the manuscript and for their enduring patience and understanding.

ALSO BY ALAN LIGHTMAN

THE DIAGNOSIS

From Alan Lightman comes this harrowing tale of one man's struggle to cope in a wired world, even as his own biological wiring short-circuits. As Boston's Red Line shuttles Bill Chalmers to work one summer morning, something extraordinary happens. Suddenly, he can't remember which stop is his, where he works, or even who he is. The only thing he can remember is his corporate motto: the maximum information in the minimum time. Bill's memory returns, but a strange numbness afflicts him. As he attempts to find a diagnosis for his deteriorating illness, he descends into a nightmarish tangle of inconclusive results, his company's manic frenzy, and his family's disbelief. Ultimately, Bill discovers that he is fighting not just for his body but for his soul.

Fiction/Literature/0-375-72550-4

EINSTEIN'S DREAMS

A modern classic, *Einstein's Dreams* is a fictional collage of stories dreamed by Albert Einstein in 1905, when he worked in a patent office in Switzerland. As the defiant but sensitive young genius is creating his theory of relativity, a new conception of time, he imagines many possible worlds. In one, time is circular, so that people are fated to repeat triumphs and failures over and over. In another, there is a place where time stands still, visited by lovers and parents clinging to their children. In another, time is a nightingale, sometimes trapped by a bell jar. Now translated into thirty languages, *Einstein's Dreams* has inspired playwrights, dancers, musicians, and painters all over the world. In poetic vignettes, it explores the connections between science and art, the process of creativity, and ultimately the fragility of human existence.

Fiction/Literature/1-4000-7780-X